Classics.

THE LAST OF THE MOHICANS

J. FENIMORE COOPER

Abbey Classics

© **Brown Watson** (Leicester) Ltd.

1

A RISKY JOURNEY

It was a feature peculiar to the colonial wars of North America between the French and the English that the toils and dangers of the wilderness were to be encountered before the adverse hosts could meet.

Perhaps no district throughout the wide extent of the intermediate frontiers can furnish a livelier picture of the cruelty and fierceness of the savage warfare of those periods than the country which lies between the head-waters of the Hudson and the adjacent lakes. A wide and apparently an impervious boundary of forests severed the possessions of the hostile provinces of France and England. The hardy colonist and the trained European who fought at his side frequently expended months in struggling against the rapids of the streams or the rugged passes of the mountains in quest of an opportunity to exhibit their courage against their hard-found foes.

The facilities which nature had there offered to the march of the combatants were too obvious to be neglected. The lengthened sheet of Lake Champlain stretched from the frontiers of Canada deep within the borders of the neighbouring province of New York, forming a natural passage across half the distance that the French were compelled to master in order to strike their enemies. Near its southern termination it received the contributions of another lake, named the 'Holy Lake' by Jesuit missionaries, while the less zealous English called it 'Lake George' after the name of their reigning prince, George, the second of the House of Hanover. The two united to oust its original Indian name of 'Horican.

Winding its way among countless islands, and embedded in mountains, the Holy Lake extended a dozen leagues still farther to the south. With the high plain that there interposed itself to the farther passage of the water commenced a portage of as many miles, which conducted the adventurer to the banks of the Hudson at a point where, with the usual obstruction of the rapids or rifts, as they were then termed in the language of the country, the river became navigable to the tide.

This area became the bloody arena in which most of the battles for the mastery of the colony were contested. Forts were erected at the different points that commanded the facilities of the route, and were taken and retaken, razed and rebuilt as victory alighted on the hostile banners. Armies were seen to bury themselves in these forests, whence they rarely returned but in skeleton bands that were haggard with care or dejected by defeat. It was amid such strife and bloodshed that the incidents we shall attempt to relate occurred, during the third year of the war which England and France last waged for the possession of a country that neither was destined to retain.

At this time the southern termination of the portage between the Hudson and Lake George was covered b᾿ an English fort known as Fort Edward after a favourite prince of the reigning family. Here lay General Webb who commanded the armies of the King in the northern provinces with a body of more than five thousand men. On the shore of Lake George, at the northern termination of the portage, was the forest fastness known as Fort William Henry, held by the veteran Scotsman Munro with a regiment of regulars and a few provincials. When this latter passed on to General Webb the intelligence that Montcalm had been seen moving up Lake Champlain with an army 'numerous as the leaves on the trees,' its truth was admitted with more fear than with the stern joy

4

that a warrior should feel in finding an enemy within reach of his blow.

The Indian runner who brought the news also bore an urgent request from Munro for a speedy and powerful reinforcement, his force being really far too small to make head against the formidable power of Montcalm.

On receipt of the news Webb gave orders that a chosen detachment of fifteen hundred men was to depart with the dawn for Fort William Henry at the northern extremity of the portage, and next morning the column of men set out. The distance between these two ports was less than five leagues. The rude path which originally formed their line of communication had been widened for the passage of wagons, so that the distance might easily be effected by a detachment of troops with their necessary baggage, between the rising and the setting of a summer sun.

Next morning, the deepest sounds of the retiring and invisible column had ceased to be born on the breeze to the listeners, and the latest straggler had already disappeared in pursuit, but there still remained the signs of another departure. Before a log cabin of unusual size and accommodations, were gathered some half-dozen horses, caparisoned in a manner which showed that two at least were destined to bear the persons of females of a rank that it was not usual to meet so far in the wilds of the country. A third, a high-mettled military charger, wore the trappings and arms of an officer of the staff. At a respectful distance were gatherd divers groups of curious idlers. There was one man among the group of bystanders, however, who by his countenance and actions formed a marked exception to those who composed the latter class of spectators, being neither idle nor semingly very ignorant.

The person of this individual was to the last degree ungainly without being in any particular manner deformed. He had all the bones and joints of other men without any of their proportions. Erect, his stature surpassed that of his fellows, though, seated he appeared reduced within the ordinary limits of the race. His head was large, his shoulders narrow, his arms long and dangling, while his hands were small if not delicate. His legs and thighs were thin almost to emaciation, but of extraordinary length. The ill-assorted and injudicious attire of the individual only served to render his awkwardness more conspicuous. A sky-blue coat, with short and broad skirts and low cape, exposed a long thin neck and longer and thinner legs. His nether garment was of yellow nankeen, closely fitted to the shape and tied to his bunches of knees by large knots of white riband a good deal sullied by use. Clouded cotton stockings and shoes, on one of the latter of which was a plated spur, completed the costume of the lower extremity of this figure. From beneath the flap of an enormous pocket of a soiled vest of embossed silk heavily ornamented with tarnished silver lace, projected an instrument which, from being seen in such martial company, might have been easily mistaken for some mischievous and unknown implement of war. A large civil cocked hat, like those worn by clergymen within the last thirty years, surmounted the whole, furnishing dignity to a good-natured and somewhat vacant countenance that apparently needed such artificial aid to support the gravity of some high and extraordinary trust.

While the common herd stood aloof in deference to the quarters of Webb, the figure we have described stalked into the centre of the domestics, freely expressing his censures or commendations on the merits of the horses as by chance they displeased or satisfied his judgement. His comments were interspersed with many quotations from Holy writ.

He turned to the silent, still, upright and rigid form of the Indian runner who had born to the camp the unwelcome tidings of the preceding evening. Although in a state of perfect repose, and apparently disregarding, with characteristic stoicism, the excitement and bustle around him, there was a sullen fierceness mingled with the quiet of the savage that was likely to arrest the attention of much more experienced eyes than those which now scanned him in unconcealed amazement. The native bore the tomahawk and knife of his tribe; and yet his appearance was not altogether that of a warrior. On the contrary, there was an air of neglect about his person, like that which might have proceeded from great and recent exertion, which he had not yet found leisure to repair. The colours of the war paint had blended in dark confusion about his fierce countenance, and rendered his swarthy lineaments still more savage and repulsive than if art had attempted an effect which had been thus produced by chance. His eye alone which glistened like a fiery star amid lowering clouds, was to be seen in its state of native wildness.

As the searching yet wary glance of the one met the wondering look of the other, a low sound of gentle voices announced the approach of those whose presence was alone wanted to enable the cavalcade to move, and a young man in the dress of an officer conducted to their steed two ladies, who, as it was apparent by their dresses, were prepared to encounter the fatigues of a journey in the woods. One, and she was the most juvenile in appearance, though both were young, permitted glimpses of her dazzling complexion, fair golden hair and bright blue eyes, to be caught as she artlessly suffered the morning air to blow aside the green veil which descended low from her beaver. There was nothing more bright nor delicate than the bloom on her cheek, nor more cheering than the animated smile which she bestowed on the youth as he assisted her into the saddle. The other, who appeared to share equally in the attentions of the young officer, concealed her charms with a care fitted to the experience of four or five additional years. It could be seen, however, that her person was rather fuller and more mature than that of her companion.

No sooner were these ladies seated than their attendant sprang lightly into the saddle of the war horse, when the whole three bowed to Webb, who in courtesy, awaited their parting on the threshold of his cabin, and turning their horses' heads they proceeded at a slow amble, followed by their train towards the northern entrance of the encampment. The Indian runner glided by and led the way along the military road in front. The veil of the older lady opened its fold momentarily and betrayed an indescribable look of pity, admiration and horror as her dark eyes followed the easy motions of the savage. The tresses of this lady were shining and black like the plumage of a raven. Her complexion was not brown but it rather appeared charged with the colour of the rich blood that seemed ready to burst its bounds. And yet there was neither coarseness nor want of shadowing in a countenance that was exquisitely regular and dignified and surpassingly beautiful. She smiled, as if in pity at her momentary forgetfulness, discovering by the act a row of teeth that would have shamed the purest ivory.

Meanwhile the younger lady inquired of the young officer who rode by her side:

'Are such spectres as that Indian frequent in the woods, Heyward; or is this sight a special entertainment ordered on behalf of Cora and myself?'

'Yon Indian is a runner of the army; and after the fashion of his people he may be accounted a hero', returned the officer. 'He has volunteered to guide us to the fort on Lake George, by a path but little known, sooner than if we followed the tardy movements of the column.'

'I like him not,' said the lady, shuddering, partly in assumed, yet more in real terror. 'You know him, Duncan, or you would not trust yourself so freely to his keeping.'

'Say, rather, Alice, that I would not trust you. I do know him or he would not have my confidence. He is said to be a Canadian and yet he served with our friends the Mohawks, who, as you know, are one of the six allied Indian Tribes. He was brought amongst us, as I have heard, by some strange accident in which your father was interested, and in which the savage was rigidly dealt by—but I forget the idle tale; it is enough that he is now our friend.'

'If he has been my father's enemy, I like him still less! exclaimed the now really anxious girl. 'Will you not speak to him, Major Heyward, that I may hear his tones?'

'It would be vain; and answered, most probably, by an ejaculation. But he stops; the private path by which we are to journey is doubtless at hand.'

When they reached the spot where the Indian stood, pointing into the thicket that fringed the military road, a narrow and blind path which might, with some little inconvenience, receive one person at a time, became visible.

'Here then lies our way,' said the young man in a low voice. 'Manifest no distrust or you may invite the danger which you appear to apprehend.'

'Cora, what think you?' asked the reluctant fair one, turning to her older sister. 'If we journey with the troops, though we may find their presence irksome, shall we not feel better assurance of our safety?'

'Being little accustomed to the practices of the savages, Alice, you mistake the place of real danger,' said Heyward. 'If enemies have reached the portage at all, a thing by no means probable, as our scouts are abroad, they will surely be found skirting the column, where scalps abound the most. The route of the detachment is known, while ours, having been determined within the hour, must still be secret.'

'Should we distrust the man because his manners are not our manners, and that his skin is dark?' coldly asked Cora.

Alice hesitated no longer, but giving her Narraganset horse a smart cut with the whip, she was the first to dash aside the slight branches of the bushes

9

and to follow the runner along the dark and tangled pathway.

The youth had turned to speak to the dark-eyed Cora, when the distant sound of horses' hoofs, clattering over the broken roots of the way in his rear, caused him to check his charger, and the whole party came to a halt.

In another instant the person of the ungainly man described earlier came into view on a low gaunt switch-tailed mare with as much rapidity as he could excite his meagre beast to endure.

The frown which had gathered round the handsome, open, and manly brow of Heyward gradually relaxed, and his lips curled into a slight smile, as he regarded the stranger. Alice made no very powerful effort to control her merriment, and even the dark thoughtful eye of Cora lighted with a humour that, it would seem, the habit rather than the nature of its mistress repressed.

'Seek you any here?' demanded Heyward, when the other had arrived sufficiently nigh to abate his speed; 'I trust you are no messenger of evil tidings.'

'Oh no,' replied the stranger 'I hear you are riding to William Henry. As I am journeying thitherward myself I concluded good company would seem consistent to the wishes of both parties,'

'If you journey to the lake you have mistaken your route,' said Heyward haughtily; 'the highway thither is at least half a mile behind you.'

'Even so,' returned the stranger, nothing daunted by this cold reception; 'I have tarried at Fort Edward a week. It is not prudent for anyone of my profession to be too familiar with those he has to instruct; for which reason I follow not the line of the army. Besides which, I conclude that a gentleman of your character has the best judgement in matters of wayfaring; I have, therefore, decided to join company in order that the ride may be made agreeable, and partake of social communion.'

10

'A most arbitary, if not a hasty decision!' exclaimed Heyward, undecided whether to give vent to his growing anger or to laugh in the other's face. 'But you speak of instruction and of a profession; you are an adjunct to the provincial corps as a master of the noble science of offence and defence? Or perhaps you are one who draws lines and angles under the pretence of expounding the mathematics?'

The stranger regarded his interrogator a moment and answered:

'Of offence, I hope, there is none to either party; of defence I make none. I lay claim to no higher gift than a small insight into the glorious art of petitioning and thanksgiving as practised in psalmody.'

'The man is most manifestly a disciple of Apollo,' cried the amused Alice, 'and I take him under my own especial protection. This strange man amuses me and if he has "music in his soul" let us not churlishly reject his company.' She pointed persuasively along the path with her riding whip. 'I am glad to encounter thee, friend,' continued the maiden, waving her hand to the stranger to proceed, as she urged her Narraganset to renew its amble.

They discoursed on the subject of music and the stranger declared that he limited his efforts to sacred song, and produced a psalm book from his pocket, telling Alice that he carried it with him always.

'Tis the sixth and twentieth edition,' he declared, 'promulgated at Boston, Anno Domini 1744, and is entitled: "The Psalms, Hymns and Spiritual Songs of the Old and New Testaments, faithfully translated into the English metre for the Use, Edification and Comfort of the Saints in Public and Private especially in New England."'

The stranger then opened the book and fitted a pair of iron-rimmed spectacles to his nose. Without circumlocution of apology, first pronouncing the word 'Standish', and placing the unknown instrument already described to his mouth, from which he drew a high, shrill sound that was followed by an octave

11

below from his own voice, he commenced singing the following words in full, sweet melodious tones that set the music, the poetry and the uneasy motion of his ill-trained beast at defiance:

"How good it is, O see,
And how it pleaseth well,
Together e'en in unity,
For brethren so to dwell.

It's like the choice ointment,
From the head to th' beard did go:
Down Aarcu s beard that downward went,
His garment's skirts unot.'

As the singing reached the ears of those in front, the Indian muttered a few words in broken English to Heyward and he in turn closed the stranger's musical efforts.

'Common prudence would teach us to journey through this wilderness in as quiet a manner as possible. You will—'

He broke off sharply and turned his head towards a thicket; then bent his eyes suspiciously on their guide. As he, however, continued his steady pace in undisturbed gravity, the young man smiled to himself for he believed he had mistaken some shining berry of the woods for the glistening eyeballs of a prowling savage.

But Major Heyward had not been mistaken. The cavalcade had not long passed, before the branches of the bushes that formed the thicket were cautiously moved asunder, and a human visage, as fiercely wild as savage art and unbridled passions could make it, peered out on the retiring footsteps of the travellers. A gleam of exultation shot across the darkly painted lineaments of the inhabitant of the forest as he traced the route of his intended victims.

2

A TREACHEROUS GUIDE

Leaving the unsuspecting Heyward and his confiding companions the scene shifts a few miles to the westward.

On that day two men were lingering on the banks of a small but rapid stream, within an hour's journey of the encampment of Webb, like those who waited the appearance of an absent person or the approach of some expected event.

While one of these loiterers showed the red skin and wild accoutrements of a native of the woods, the other exhibited through the mask of his rude and nearly savage equipments, the brighter, though sunburnt and long-faded complexion of one who might claim descent from a European parentage. The body of the former, which was nearly naked, presented a terrific emblem of death, drawn in intermingled colours of white and black. His closely shaved head on which no other hair than the well-known and chivalrous scalping-tuft was preserved, was without ornament of any kind with the exception of a solitary eagle's plume which crossed his crown and depended over the left shoulder. A tomahawk and scalping knife of English manufacture were in his girdle while a short military rifle of that sort with which the policy of the whites armed their savage allies, lay carelessly across his bare and sinewy knee. The expanded chest, full-formed limbs and grave countenance of this warrior would denote that he had reached the vigour of his days, though no symptoms of decay appeared to have yet weakened his manhood.

The frame of the white man, judging by such parts as were not concealed by his clothes, was like that of one who had known hardships and exertion from his earliest youth. He wore a hunting shirt of forest green fringed with faded yellow, and a summer cap of skins that had been shorn of their fur. He also bore a knife in a girdle of wampum like that which confined the scanty garments of the Indian, but no tomahawk. His moccasins were ornamented after the gay fashion of the natives, while the only part of his underdress which appeared below the hunting frock was a pair of buckskin leggings that laced at the sides and were gartered above the knees with the sinews of a deer. A pouch and horn completed his personal accoutrements, though a hunting rifle of great length, which the theory of the more ingenious whites had taught them was the most dangerous of all firearms, leaned against a neighbouring sapling. The eye of the hunter, or scout, whichever he might be, was small, quick, keen and restless, roving even as he spoke, on every side of him, as if in search of game or distrusting the sudden approach of some lurking enemy.

'Even your traditions make the case in my favour, Chingachgook,' he said, speaking in the tongue which was known to all the natives who formerly inhabited the country between the Hudson and the Potomack. 'Your fathers came from the setting sun, crossed the Mississippi river, fought the red people of the country and took the land; and mine came from the red sky of the morning over the salt lake and did their work much after the fashion that had been set them by yours; then let God judge the matter between us, and friends spare their words! But every story has two sides; so I ask you, Chingachgook, what passed, according to the traditions of the red man, when our fathers first met?'

'Listen, Hawk-eye,' returned the Indian sternly, 'and your ear shall drink no lie.' 'Tis what my fathers have said, and what the Mohicans have done. First my fathers fought with the naked red man. We came from the place where the sun is hid at night, over great plains where the buffaloes live, until we reached the big river. There we fought the Alligewi till the ground was red with their blood. From the banks of the big river to the shores of the salt lake there was none to meet us. The Maquas followed at a distance. The land we had taken like warriors we kept like men, we drove the Maquas into the woods with the bears. They only tasted salt at the licks; they drew us fish from the great lake; we threw them the bones.'

'All this I have heard and believe,' said the white man, 'but it was long before the English came into the country.'

'Yes, the first pale faces who came among us spoke no English. They came in a large canoe when my father had buried the tomahawk with the red men around them. Then, Hawk-eye,' continued the Indian with deep emotion, 'we were one people and we were happy. The salt lake gave us its fish, the wood its deer, and the air its birds. We took wives who bore us children, we worshipped the Great Spirit, and we kept the Maquas beyond the sound of our songs of triumph.'

'Know you anything of your own family at that time?' demanded the white. 'You hold their gifts; your fathers must have been brave warriors and wise men at the council fire.'

'My tribe is the grandfather of nations, but I am an unmixed man. The blood of chiefs is in my veins, where it must stay forever. The Dutch landed and gave my people the fire-water; they drank until the heavens and the earth seemed to meet, and they foolishly thought they had found the Great Spirit. Then they parted with their land. Foot by foot they were driven back from the shores until I, that am a chief and a Sagamore, have never visited the graves of my fathers!'

'But where are to be found those of your race who came to their kin in the Delaware country, so many summers since?' asked Hawk-eye.

'Where are the blossoms of those summers?—Fallen, one by one; so all of my family departed, each in turn, to the land of spirits. I am on the hill-top, and must go down to the valley; and when my boy Uncas follows in my footsteps, there will be no longer any of the blood of the Sagamores for Uncas is the last of the Mohicans.'

'Uncas is here!' said another voice, in the same, soft, gutteral tones near his elbow. 'Who speaks to Uncas?'

At the next instant a youthful warrior passed between them with a noiseless step and seated himself on the bank of the rapid stream. Chingachgook turned his eyes slowly towards his son and demanded:

'Do the Maquas dare to leave the print of their moccasins in those woods?'

'I have been on their trail,' replied the young Indian, 'and know they number as many as the fingers of my two hands; but they lie hid like cowards'

'The thieves are out lying for scalps and plunder!' said the white man. 'That busy Frenchman, Montcalm will send his spies into our very camp, but he will know what road we travel!'

'"Tis enough!' returned the father. 'They shall be driven like deer from the bushes. But listen! I hear the sounds of feet! The horses of white men are coming! Hawk-eye, they are your brothers. Speak to them.'

'That will I, and in English that the king needn't be ashamed to answer', returned the hunter, speaking in the language of which he boasted. 'Ha! Now I hear the bushes move—yes, yes there is a trampling that I mistook for the falls—and—but here they come themselves. God keep them from the Iroquois!'

A moment later the leader of the party, whose approaching footsteps had caught the vigilant ear of the Indian, came openly into view.

'Who comes?' demanded Hawk-eye, throwing his rifle carelessly across his left arm, and keeping the forefinger of his right hand on the trigger, though he avoided all appearance of menace in the act. 'Who

16

comes hither among the beasts and dangers of the wilderness, and on what account?'

'Men who have journeyed since the rising sun in the shades of this forest, without nourishment and are sadly tired of their wayfaring,' returned he who rode foremost. 'Know you the distance to a post of the crown called William Henry?'

'Hoot!' shouted Hawk-eye. 'You are as much off the scent as a hound would be with Horican atwixt him and the deer!'

'It is enough at the present that we trusted to an Indian guide to take us by a nearer, though blinder path, and that we are deceived in his knowledge. In plain words, we know not where we are,' returned Heyward, for it was he.

'An Indian lost in the woods!' said Hawk-eye, shaking his head doubtingly. 'Tis strange that an Indian should be lost atwixt Horican and the bend in the river. Is he a Mohawk?'

'Not by birth, though adopted in that tribe; I think his birthplace was farther north, and he is one of those you call a Huron.'

'A Huron!' repeated the other, once more shaking his head in open distrust. 'They are a thievish race, nor do I care by whom they are adopted; you can never make anything of them but skulks and vagabonds. Since you trusted yourself to the care of one of that nation, I only wonder that you have not fallen in with more.'

'Of that there is little danger since William Henry is so many miles in our front. You forget that I have told you our guide is now a Mohawk and that he serves our forces as a friend.'

'And I tell you that he who is born a Mingo, will die a Mingo,' returned the other positively. 'A Mohawk! No, trust him not, look to a Delaware, or a Mohican for honesty!'

'Enough of this,' said Heyward impatiently; then, speaking in a more gentle voice: 'If you will tell me the distance to Fort Edward, and conduct me thither, your labour shall not go without its reward.'

'And in so doing, how know I that I don't guide an enemy and a spy of Montcalm to the works of the army? It is not every man who can speak the English tongue that is an honest subject.'

'If you serve with the troops, of whom I judge you to be scout, you should know of such a regiment of the king as the 60th, and the youngest of its majors.'

'Yes, I have heard that a young gentleman of vast riches, from one of the provinces far south has got the place. He is over young too, to hold such rank, and to be put above men whose heads are beginning to bleach; and yet they say he is a soldier in his knowledge and a gallant gentleman!'

'He now speaks to you and, of course, can be no enemy to dread.'

Hawk-eye regarded Heyward in surprise, then, lifting his cap, he answered, in a tone less confident than before, though expressing doubt:

'I have heard a party was to leave the encampment this morning for the lake shore?'

'You have heard the truth, but I preferred a nearer route, trusting to the knowledge of the Indian 1 mentioned.'

'And he deceived you and then deserted?'

'Neither, as I believe; certainly not the latter for he is to be found in the rear.'

'I should like to look at the creature; if it is a true Iroquis I can tell by his knavish look and by his paint,' said Hawk-eye, entering the path behind the mare of the singing master.

Returning to Heyward he shook his head and declared:

'A Mingo is a Mingo, and God having made him so, neither the Mohawks nor any other tribe can alter him,' he said when he had regained his former position. 'I wouldn't walk a mile in these woods, after night gets into them, in company with that runner, for the best rifle in the colonies. They are full of outlying

Iroquois, and your mongrel Mohawk knows too well where to find them to be my companion.'

'Think you so?' said Heyward, leaning forward in the saddle, and dropping his voice nearly to a whisper. 'I confess I have not been without my suspicions.'

'I knew he was one of the cheats as soon as I laid eyes on him,' returned the other, placing a finger on his nose in sign of caution. Then, after musing a moment he made a gesture which instantly brought his two red companions to his side. They spoke together in the Delaware language whereupon the two Indians, after laying aside their firearms, parted, taking opposite sides of the path, and burying themselves in the thicket with such cautious movements that their steps were inaudible.

'Now, go you back,' said Hawk-eye to Heyward, 'and hold the imp in talk; these Mohicans here will take him. Talk openly to the miscreant and seem to believe him the truest friend on earth. He must suspect nothing.'

Heyward prepared to comply, though with strong disgust at the nature of the office.

'You may see, Magua,' he said to his Indian guide, endeavouring to assume an air of freedom and confidence, 'that the night is closing around us and yet we are no nearer to William Henry than when we left the encampment of Webb with the rising sun. You have missed the way, not have I been more fortunate. But happily we have fallen in with a hunter, he whom you now hear talking to the singer, that is acquainted with the deer-paths and by-ways of the woods, and who promises to lead us to a place where we may rest till the morning.'

The Indian riveted his glowing eyes on Heyward as he asked, in his imperfect English: 'Is he alone?'

'Alone!' hesitatingly answered Heyward, to whom deception was too new to be assumed without embarrassment. 'Oh, not alone, surely, Magua, for you know that we are with him.'

'Then Le Renard Subtil will go', returned the runner, coolly raising his wallet from the place where it had lain at his feet, 'and the pale-faces will see none but their own colour.'

'Go! Whom call you Le Renard?'

"'Tis the name his Canada fathers have given to Magua,' returned the runner, with an air that manifested his pride at the destinction.

Heyward now felt it had become incumbent on him to act. Throwing his leg over the saddle he dismounted, with a determination to advance and seize his treacherous companion, trusting the result to his own manhood. In order, however, to prevent unnecessary alarm, he still preserved an air of calmness and friendship.

'Le Renard Subtil does not eat,' he said, using the appellation he had found most flattering to the vanity of the Indian. 'His corn is not well parched and it seems dry. Let me examine; perhaps something may be found among my own provisions that will help his appetite.'

Magua held out the wallet to the proffer of the other. He even suffered their hands to meet, without betraying the least emotion or varying his riveted attitude of attention. But when he felt the finger of Heyward moving gently along his own naked arms he struck up the limb of the young man, and uttering a piercing cry as he darted beneath it, plunged at a single bound into the opposite thicket. At the next instant the form of Chingachgook appeared from the bushes, looking like a spectre in its paint, and glided across the path in swift pursuit. Next followed the shout of Uncas, when the woods were lighted by a sudden flash, that was accompanied by the sharp report of the hunter's rifle.

3

ATTACKED BY THE MAQUAS

The suddenness of the flight and the wild cries of
his pursuers caused Heyward to remain fixed for a
few moments in inactive surprise. Then, recollecting
the importance of securing the fugitive, he dashed
aside the surrounding bushes and pressed eagerly
forward to lend his aid in the chase. Before he had,
however, proceeded a hundred yards, he met the
three foresters already returning from their unsuccessful
pursuit.

'Why so soon disheartened!' he exclaimed. 'The
scoundrel must be concealed behind some of these
trees, and may yet be secured. We are not safe while
he goes at large,'

'Would you set a cloud to chase the wind?' asked
the disappointed hunter. 'I heard the imp brushing
over the dry leaves like a black snake, and blinking
a glimpse of him just over agin yon big pine I pulled
as it might be, on the scent; but t'wouldn't do. I
rubbed the bark of a limb perhaps, but the creature
leapt the longer for it.'

'We are four able bodies to one wounded man!'

'Is life grievous to you?' interrupted Hawk-eye.
'Yonder red devil would draw you within swing of
the tomahawks of his comrades before you were heated
in the chase. It was unthoughtful of myself who has
so often slept with the war-whoop ringing in the air
to let off my piece within sound of an ambushment.
But then it was a natural temptation; just as 'twas
very natural for you not to have left it to the two

Mohicans to take the scoundrel, as I directed you. Come, friends, let us move our station, and in such a fashion, too, as will throw the cunning of 9 Mingo on a wrong scent, or our scalps will be dryin ain the wind in front of Montcalm's marquee this hour tomorrow.'

This appalling declaration which the scout uttered with the cool assurance of a man who fully comprehended, while he did not fear to face, the danger, served to remind Heyward of the importance of the charge with which he himself had been entrusted.

'What is to be done?' he said, feeling the utter helplessness of doubt in such a pressing straight. 'Desert me not for God's sake! Remain to defend those defenceless creatures I escort, and freely name your own reward!'

'It would not be the act of men to leave such harmless things to their fate,' answered Hawk-eye. 'If you would save these tender blossoms from the fangs of the worst of serpents, gentleman, you have neither time to lose nor resolution to throw away. But spare your offers of money. These Mohicans and I will do what man's thoughts can invent to keep from harm such flowers, which, though sweet, were never made for the wilderness. Now follow, for we are losing moments that are as precious as the heart's blood to a stricken deer.'

Quickly Heyward told the two ladies of the danger of their position and they braced their nerves to undergo some unlooked-for and unusual trial; then, having d smounted, they suffered the two Indians to take their horses' bridles and to lead the frightened and reluctant animals into the bed of the river. Shuddering and clinging closer to one another, the sisters watched them all move a short distance from the shore, then turn and continue upstream until they were concealed by the projection of the bank.

'The Indians will hide the beasts with the judgement of natives,' explained the scout. 'They will be secured to some scattering shrubs that grow in the hidden fissures of the rocks. There they can be left to spend the night, standing in the water. Water leaves no trail.'

The scout now drew a canoe of bark from its place of concealment in some low bushes and directed Heyward and his disconsolate fellow-travellers to seat themselves in the forward end of it, while he took possession of the other himself, as erect and steady as if he floated in a vessel of much firmer materials; then, placing his pole against a rock, by a powerful shove he sent his frail bark directly into the centre of the turbulent stream.

The travellers cast many a fearful and anxious glance around them. The river was confined between high and craggy rocks; these, being surmounted by tall trees which appeared to totter on the brow of the precipice, gave the stream the appearance of running through a deep and narrow chasm. In front, the dull but increasing roar of a waterfall filled them with terror that was doubled as they beheld the water ahead piling against the heavens.

For many minutes the struggle between the light bubble in which they floated and the swift current was severe and doubtful. Twenty times they thought she swirling eddies were sweeping them to destruction but always the masterhand of their pilot would bring the bows of the canoe to stem the rapids. At last, just as Alice veiled her eyes in horror under the impression that they were about to be swept within the vortex at the foot of the cataract, the canoe floated stationary at the foot of a flat rock that lay on a level with the water, while on either side of them there thundered a mighty cascade.

'Where are we? And what is next to be done?' demanded Heyward, perceiving that the exertions of the scout had ceased.

'You are at the foot of Glenn's Fall' returned the other, speaking aloud, without fear of consequences, within the roar of the cataract; 'and the next thing is to make a steady landing. There go you all on the rock, and I will go back and bring up the Mohicans with the venison; a man had better sleep without his scalp than famish amidst plenty.'

Left by their guide, the travellers remained for a time in helpless ignorance of their fate, but their suspense was soon relieved; for aided by the skill of the natives, the canoe shot back into the eddy, and floated again at the side of the low rock.

'We are now fortified, garrisoned and provisioned,' cried Heyward cheerfully, 'and may set Montcalm and his allies at defiance. How now, my vigilant sentinel, can you see anything of those you call the Iroquois on the mainland?'

'I call them Iroquois because to me every native who speaks a foreign tongue is accounted an enemy, though he may pretend to serve the king. If Webb wants faith and honesty in an Indian, let him bring out the tribes of the Delawares and send these greedy and lying Mohawks and Oneidas with their six nations of varlets, where in nature they belong, among the French!'

The scout, whilst making his remarks, was busied in collecting certain implements; as he concluded he moved silently among the group of travellers, accompanied by the Mohicans, who seemed to comprehend his intentions with instinctive readiness; then the whole three disappeared in succession, seeming to vanish against the dark face of a perpendicular rock that rose to the height of a few yards, within as many feet of the water's edge. Only by moving after them straight up to the rock face, did Heyward and his companions find there the cunningly concealed embrasure to a cave and follow their guides inside.

At the farther extremity of a narrow, deep cavern in the rock, the scout had already busied himself stirring a fire into life. Beside him was Chingachgook and a little distance in advance stood Uncas, his whole person thrown powerfully into view. The travellers anxiously regarded the upright, flexible figure of the young Mohican, graceful and unrestrained in the attitudes and movements of nature. Though his person was more than usually screened by a green and fringed hunting shirt like that of the white man, there was no concealment to his dark glancing, fearless eye, alike terrible and calm; the bold outline of his high haughty features, pure in their native red; or to the dignified elevation of his receding forehead together with all the finest proportions of a noble head, bared to the generous scalping tuft.

'I could sleep in peace,' whispered Alice, nodding in the direction of Uncas, 'with such a fearless and generous-looking youth for my sentinel.'

A short silence succeeded this remark, which was interrupted by the scout.

'This fire begins to show too bright a flame,' he called out, 'and might light the Mingoes to our undoing. Uncas, drop the blanket and show the knaves its dark side. This is not such a supper as a major of the Royal Americans has a right to expect, but I have known stout detachments of the corps glad to eat their venison raw, and without a relish too.'

Uncas did as the other had directed, and, when the voice of Hawk-eye ceased, the roar of the cataract sounded like the rumbling of distant thunder.

'Are we safe in this cavern?' demanded Heyward. 'Is these no danger of suprise? A single armed man at its entrance would hold us at his mercy.'

For answer, Chingachgook seized a blazing brand and held it towards the farther extremity of their place of retreat. At that point, lifting another blanket, he revealed that the cavern had two outlets. Then, holding the brand, he crossed a deep narrow chasm in the rocks, which ran at right-angles with the passage they were in, but which, unlike that, was open to the heavens, and entered another cave answering to the description of the first in every particular.

'Such old foxes as Chingachgook and myself are not often caught in a burrow with one hole,' said Hawk-eye, laughing. 'You can easily see the cunning of the place here amidst the cataract. The rock is black limestone, which everyone knows is soft, and where there have been cracks in the rock, the water has worked out deep hollows for itself, amongst them these two little holes for us to hide in. The rock too, on each side of us has proved softer, and being worn away has left this core in the middle of the cataract, bare and dry.'

'We are then on an island?'

'Ay! There are the falls on two sides of us and the river above and below. If you had daylight it would be worth the trouble to step up on the height of this rock and look at the perversity of the water. It falls by no rule at all; sometimes it leaps, sometimes it tumbles; there it skips, there it shoots; in one place 'tis white as snow, and in another 'tis green as grass; hereabouts it pitches into deep hollows that rumble and quake the earth, and thereaway it ripples and sings like a brook, fashioning whirlpools and gulleys in the stone as if it were no harder than trodden clay.'

While his auditors received a cheering assurance of the security of their place of concealment from this untutored description of Glenn's Falls, they were much inclined to judge differently from Hawk-eye of its wild beauties, but they suffered their attention to be drawn from their thoughts to the necessary though more vulgar consideration of their supper. In the course of a refreshing repast of venison, they learned that the singing master who accompanied them was called David Gamut, and that he instructed the youths of the Connecticut levy in the art of psalmody. At the end of the meal, he offered to lead the company in the singing of a psalm of praise after such a day of jeopardy, and the singers were dwelling on one of those low dying chords which the ear devours with such greedy rapture, when a cry that seemed neither human nor earthly rose in the outward air, penetrating not only the recesses of the cavern but to the inmost hearts of all that heard it. It was followed by a deep stillness.

'What is it?' murmured Alice, after a few moments of terrible suspense.

Neither Hawk-eye nor the Indians made any reply. They listened as if expecting the sound would be repeated, with a manner that expressed their own astonishment. At length they spoke together earnestly in the Delaware language; then Uncas passing by the inner and most concealed aperture, cautiously left the cavern. When he had gone, the scout spoke in English.

'What it is, or what it is not, none can tell, though two of us have ranged the woods for more than thirty years. I did believe that there was no cry that Indian or beast could make that my ears had not heard, but this has proved that I was only a vain and conceited mortal.'

'Was it not, then, the shout the warriors made when they wish to intimidate their enemies?' asked Cora, who stood drawing her veil about her person with a calmness to which her agitated sister was a stranger.

'No, no; this was bad and shocking, and had a sort of unhuman sound; but when you once hear the war-whoop you will never mistake it for anything else. Well, Uncas,' speaking in Delaware to the young chief as he re-entered, 'what see you? Do our lights shine through the blankets?'

The answer was short and apparently decided, being given in the same tongue.

'There is nothing to be seen without,' continued Hawk-eye, shaking his head in discontent, 'and our hiding place is still in darkness.'

'It is extraordinary,' said Heyward, taking his pistols from the place where he had laid them on entering. 'Be it a sign of piece or a signal of war, it must be looked into.' Come, my friends.'

On issuing from their place of confinement the whole party instantly experienced a grateful renovation of spirits, by exchanging the spent air of the hiding-place for the cool and invigorating atmosphere which played round the whirlpools and pitches of the cataract.

27

'Here is nothing to be seen but the gloom and quiet of a lovely evening,' whispered Duncan. 'How much should we prize such a scene and all this breathing solitude, at any other moment, Cora! Fancy yourselves in security and what now perhaps increases your terror may be made conducive to enjoyment...'

'Listen!' interrupted Alice.

The caution was unnecessary. Once more the same sound arose as if from the bed of the river, and, having broken out of the narrow bounds of the cliffs, was heard undulating through the forest in distant and dying cadences.

'I have it,' said Duncan. 'I know the sound full well for often have I heard it on the field of battle, and in situations which are frequent in a soldier's life. 'Tis the horrid shriek that a horse will give in his agony, oftener drawn from him in pain, though sometimes in terror. My charger is either a prey to the beasts of the forest, or sees his danger without the power to avoid it. The sound might deceive me in the cavern, but in the open air I know it too well to be wrong.'

The scout and his companions listened to this simple explanation with the interest of men who imbibe new ideas at the same time they get rid of old ones which had proved disagreeable inmates.

'I cannot deny your word', said the scout, 'for I am little skilled in horses though born where they abound. The wolves must be hovering above the heads on the bank, and the timorsome creatures are calling on man for help, in the best manner they are able. Uncas,' he spoke in Delaware— 'Uncas, drop down in the canoe and whirl a brand among the pack, or fear may do what the wolves can't get at to perform, and leave us without horses in the morning, when we shall have so much need to journey swiftly.'

The young native had already descended to the water to comply, when a long howl was raised on the edge of the river, and was borne swiftly off into the depths of the forest, as though the beasts of their own accord were abandoning their prey in sudden terror. Uncas, with instinctive quickness receded, and the three foresters held another of their low, earnest conferences.

'Pass now into the other cave, you that need it, and seek for sleep. We must be afoot long before the sun and make the most of our time to get to Fort Edward while the Mingoes are taking their morning nap.

Cora set the exemple of compliance with a steadiness that taught the more timid Alice the necessity of obedience. Then all ᴛhe men posted themselves on the rocks in the shade ᴄast by the moon from some thick beech-trees, and while Heyward and David fell asleep, Hawk-eye and the natives watched until the moon had set and a pale streak above the tree-tops, at the bend of the river below, announced the approach of day.

Then, for the first time, Hawk-eye was seen to stir. He crawled along the rock and shook Duncan from his heavy slumbers.

'Now is the time to journey,' he whispered. 'Awake the gentle ones, and be ready to get into the canoe when I bring it to the landing place. All is yet still as midnight. Be silent, but be quick.'

Duncan immediately passed into the cavern and lifted the shawl from the sleeping ladies. The motion caused Cora to raise her hand as if to repulse him, while Alice murmured in her soft gentle, voice: 'No, no, dear father, we were not deserted; Duncan was with us.'

'Yes, sweet innocence,' whispered the youth. 'Duncan is here and while life continues or danger remains he will never quit thee. Cora! Alice! Awake! The hour has come to move'. While the words were still on the lips of Heyward there had arisen such a tumult of yells and cries as served to drive the swift currents of his own blood back from its bounding course into the fountains of his heart. He dashed outside just in time to see David raise his tall person in the midst of the infernal din, with a hand on either ear, exclaiming:

'Whence comes this discord? Has hell broke loose that man should utter sounds like these?

The bright flashes and the quick reports from a dozen rifles from the opposite banks of the stream followed this incautious exposure of his person, and left the unfortunate singing master unconscious on the rock where he had been so long slumbering. In return, a stream of flame issued from the rock beneath him and a fierce yell blended with a shriek of agony announced that the messenger of death sent from the fatal weapon of Hawk-eye had found a victim. At this slight repulse the assailants instantly withdrew, and gradually the place became as still as before the sudden tumult.

Duncan seized the favourable moment to spring to the body of Gamut, which he bore within the narrow chasm which protected the sisters. In another minute the whole party was collected in this spot of comparative safety.

'The poor fellow has saved his scalp,' said Hawk-eye, coolly passing his hand over the head of David; 'but he is a proof that a man may be born with too long a tongue. 'Twas downright madness to show six feet of flesh and blood on a naked rock to the raging savages. I only wonder he has escaped with life.'

'Is he not dead?' demanded Cora in a voice whose husky tones showed how powerfully natural horror struggled with her assumed firmness. 'Can we do aught to assist the wretched man?"

'No, no, the life is in his heart yet, and after he has slept awhile he will come to himself, and be a wiser man for it, until the hour of his real time shall come', returned Hawkeye. 'Carry him in, Uncas, and lay him on the sassafras. Singing won't do any good with the Iroquois.'

'You believe then, the attack will be renewed?' asked Heyward.

'Do I expect a hungry wolf will satisfy his craving with a mouthful? They have lost a man and 'tis their fashion, when they meet a loss and fail in the surprise, to fall back; but we shall have them on again, with new ingredients to circumvent us and master our scalps.'

'You hear our probable fortunes, Cora,' said Duncan. 'Come then with Alice; remain in this cavern where you will at least be safe from the murderous rifles of our enemies, and where you may bestow a care suited to your gentle natures on our unfortunate comrade.'

'Duncan,' said the tremulous voice of Cora, 'remember, Duncan, how necessary your safety is to our own—how you bear a father's sacred trust—how much depends on your discretion and care. In short,' she added, while the tell-tale blood stole over her features, crimsoning her very temples, 'remember how very deservedly dear you are to all of the name of Munro.'

'If anything could add to my own base love of life,' said Heyward, suffering his unconscious eyes to wander to the youthful form of the silent Alice, 'it would be so kind an assurance. And now I must take my share of the fray and keep these bloodhounds at bay for a few hours.'

After the four men had silently repaired to their appointed stations, which were fissures in the rocks, whence they could command the approaches to the, foot of the falls, a long and anxious watch succeeded, but without any further evidence of a renewed attack, and Duncan began to hope that their fire had proved more fatal than had been supposed, and that their enemies had been effectually repulsed. When he ventured to utter this impression to his companion, it was met by Hawk-eye with an incredulous shake of the head and a silent gesture with the hand to a point above them where the water broke over the rocks.

Heyward lifted his head from the cover and beheld what he justly considered a prodigy of rashness and skill. The river had worn away the soft rock in such a manner as to render its first pitch less abrupt and perpendicular than is usual at waterfalls. At this point four human heads could be seen peering above a few logs of driftwood that had lodged on these naked rocks, and which had probably suggested the idea of the practicability of the hazardous undertaking.

'Stand firm for a close struggle while I fire on their rush,' So saying, Hawk-eye placed a finger in his mouth and drew a long shrill whistle, which was answered from the rocks that were guarded by the Mohicans. Duncan caught glimpses of the heads above the scattered drift-wood at this signal, but they disappeared again as suddenly as they had glanced upon his sight. A low rustling sound next drew his attention behind him, and turning his head, he beheld Uncas within a few feet, creeping to his side. Hawk-eye spoke to him in Delaware, then the young chief took his position with singular caution and undisturbed coolness. To Heyward this was a moment of feverish and impatient suspense, that ended as the woods were filled with another burst of cries, and at the signal four savages sprang from the cover of the driftwood. Heyward felt a burning desire to rush forward to meet them, so intense was the delirious anxiety of the moment, but he was restrained by the deliberate examples of the scout and Uncas. When their foes, who leapt over the black rocks that divided them with long bounds, uttering the wildest yells, were within a few rods, the rifle of Hawk-eye slowly rose among the shrubs and poured out its fatal contents. The foremost Indian bounded like a stricken deer and fell headlong among the clefts of the island.

'Now, Uncas,' cried the scout, drawing his long knife, while his quick eyes began to flash with ardour, 'take the last two of the screeching imps; of the other two we are certain!'

He was obeyed and but two enemies remained to be overcome. Heyward had given one of his pistols to Hawk-eye, and together they rushed down a little declivity towards their foes. They discharged their weapons at the same instant, and equally without success.

'I know'd it and I said it!' muttered the scout, hurling the despised little implement over the falls with bitter disdain. 'Come on, ye bloody villains, ye meet a man without a cross!'

The words were barely uttered when he encountered a savage of gigantic stature, and of the fiercest mien. At the same moment Duncan found himself engaged with the other in a similar contest of hand to hand. With ready skill Hawk-eye and his antagonist each grasped the uplifted arm of the other which held the dangerous knife and gradually exerted the power of their muscles for the mastery. At length the toughened sinews of the white man prevailed; the arm of the native slowly gave way before the increasing force of the scout who, suddenly wresting his armed hand from the grasp of his foe, drove the sharp weapon through his naked bosom to the heart. Duncan less skilful, would have been overcome by his adversary if Uncas had not come to his aid and dispatched his foe.

'To cover, to cover!' cried Hawk-eye. 'To cover for your lives; the work is but half ended!'

The young Mohican gave a shout of triumph, and, followed by Duncan, he glided up the acclivity they had descended to the combat, and sought the friendly shelter of the rocks and shrubs.

The warning call of the scout was not uttered without occasion. During the occurrence of the deadly encounter just related, the roar of the falls was unbroken by any human sound whatever. But the moment the struggle was decided, a yell arose as fierce and savage as wild and revengeful passions could throw into the air. It was followed by the swift flashes of the rifles, which sent their leaden messengers across the rocks in volleys.

A steady though deliberate return was made from the rifle of Chingachgook, who had maintained his post throughout the foray with unmoved resolution. When the triumphant shout of Uncas was borne to his ears, the gratified father raised his voice in a single responsive cry, after which his busy piece alone proved that he still guarded his pass with unwearied diligence. In this manner many minutes flew by with the swift-

33

ness of thought, the rifles of the assailants speaking at times in rattling volleys, and at others in occasional scattering shots. Though the rocks, the trees and the shrubs were cut and torn in a hundred places around the besieged, their cover was so close and so rigidly maintained that as yet David had been the only sufferer in the little band.

'Let them burn their powder,' said the deliberate scout, while bullet after bullet whizzed past the place where he securely lay. 'I fancy the imps will tire of the sport before these old stones cry out for mercy. Ah! There goes another of them,' he cried gleefully, as he bore his rifle upon a ragged oak that grew on the right bank of the river and inclined so far forward that its upper branches overhung the stream. 'There's one of them concealed in that foliage.'

A few moments later the enemy sniper fell headlong into the river, as fire flashed from Hawk-eye's rifle.

"Twas the last charge in my horn and the last bullet in my pouch', said the scout. 'Uncas, lad, go down to the canoe and bring up the big horn; it is all the powder we have left, and we shall need it to the last grain, or I am ignorant of the Mingo nature.'

The young Mohican complied, leaving the scout turning over the useless contents of his pouch, and shaking the empty horn with renewed discontent. From this unsatisfactory examination, however, he was soon called by a loud and piercing exclamation from Uncas, that sounded even to the unpractised ears of Duncan as the signal of some new and unexpected calamity.

At a short distance from the rock their little bark was to be seen floating across the eddy towards the swift current of the river, in a manner which proved that its course was directed by some hidden agent. The instant this unwelcome sight caught the eye of the scout, his rifle was levelled as if by instinct, but the barrel gave no answer to the bright sparks of the flint.

"Tis too late, 'tis too late!' Hawk-eye exclaimed, dropping the useless piece in bitter disappointment.

34

'The miscreant has struck the rapids; and, had we powder, it could hardly send the lead swifter than he goes now.'

The adventurous Huron raised his head above the shelter of the canoe and, while it glided swiftly down the stream, he waved his hand and gave forth the shout which was the known signal of success.

'What is to be done?' demanded Duncan, losing the first feeling of disappointment in a more manly desire for exertion. 'What will become of us?'

Hawk-eye made no other reply than by passing his finger around the crown of his head in a manner so significant that none who witnessed the action could mistake its meaning.

For some time they held mournful conversation with each other about their approaching death.

'Why die at all?'said Cora, advancing from the place where natural horror had, until this moment, held her riveted to the rock. 'The path is open on every side. Fly then, to the woods and call on God for succour! Go, brave men, we owe you too much already; let us no longer involve you in our hapless fortunes.'

'You but little know the craft of the Iroquois, lady, if you judge they have left the path open to the woods,' returned Hawk-eye, who, however, immediately added in his simplicity, 'The down-stream current, it is certain, might soon sweep us beyond the reach of their rifles or the sound of their voices.'

'Then try the river. Why linger to add to the number of the victims of our merciless enemies? Go to Munro and say that you left his children with a message to hasten their aid,' returned Cora, advancing nigher to the scout in her generous ardour; 'that the Hurons bear them into the northern wilds, but that by vigilance and speed they may yet be rescued. And after all, if it should please heaven that his assistance should come too late, bear to him', she continued, her voice gradually lowering, until it seemed nearly choked, 'the love, the blessings, the final prayers of his daughters, and bid him not mourn their early fate, but to look forward with humble confidence to the Christian's goal to meet his children.'

The hard, weather-beaten features of the scout began to work, and when she had ended, he dropped his chin to his hand, like a man musing profoundly on the nature of the proposal.

'There is reason in her words,' at length broke from his compressed and trembling lips. 'Ay, and they bear the spirit of Christianity. What might be right and proper in a redskin might he sinful in a man who has not even a cross in blood to plead his ignorance. Chingachgook! Uncas! Hear you the talk of the dark-eyed woman?'

He now spoke in Delaware to his companions, and his address, though calm and deliberate, seemed very decided. The elder Mohican replaced his knife and tomahawk in his girdle and moved silently to the edge of the rock which was most concealed from the banks of the river. Here he paused a moment, pointed significantly to the woods below, and saying a few words in his own language, as if indicating his intended route, he dropped into the river, and sank from before the eyes of the witnesses of his movements.

The scout delayed his departure to speak to the generous girl, whose breathing became lighter as she saw the success of her remonstrance.

'Wisdom is sometimes given to the young as well as to the old,' he said, 'and what you have spoken is wise, not to call it by a better word. If you are led into the woods, that is such of you as may be spared for a while, break the twigs on the bushes as you pass, and make the marks of your trail as broad as you can; then, if mortal eyes can see them, depend on having a friend who will follow to the ends of earth afore he deserts you.'

He gave Cora an affectionate shake of the hand, lifted his rifle, and after regarding it a moment with melancholy solicitude, laid it carefully aside, and descended to the place where Chingachgook had just disappeared. For an instant he hung suspended by the rock, and, looking about him with a countenance or peculiar care, he added bitterly: 'Had the powder held out, this disgrace could never have fallen.' Then loosening his hold, the water closed above his head, and he also became lost to view.

'Your friends have not been seen, and are now most probably in safety. Is it not time for you to follow?'

'Uncas will stay,' the young Mohican calmly answered in English.

'To increase the horror of our capture, and to diminish the chances of our release! Go, generous young man. Go! 'Tis my wish, 'tis my prayer, that you will go!'

The settled calm look of the young chief changed to an expression of gloom; but he no longer hesitated. With a noiseless step he crossed the rock and dropped into the troubled stream. After the last look at Uncas, Cora turned, and with a quivering lip addressed herself to Heyward:

'I have heard of your boasted skill in the water too, Duncan,' she said. 'Follow, then, the wise example set you by these simple and faithful beings.'

'Is such the faith that Cora Munro would extract from her protector?' said the young man, smiling mournfully, but with bitterness.

'This is not a time for idle subtleties and false opinions,' she answered, 'but a moment when every duty should be equally considered. To us you can be of no further service here, but your precious life may be saved for other and nearer friends.'

'There are evils worse than death,' said Duncan, speaking hoarsely and as if fretful at her importunity, 'but which the presence of one who would die on your behalf may avert.'

Cora ceased her entreaties, and, veiling her face in her shawl, drew the nearly insensible Alice after her into the deepest recesses of the inner cavern.

4

CAPTIVES OF MAGUA

The sudden and almost magical change from the stirring incidents of the combat to the stillness that now reigned around him acted on the heated imagination of Heyward like some exciting dream. He began to rally his faculties to renewed exertions with something like a reviving confidence of success.

'The Hurons are not to be seen,' he said addressing David, who had by no means recovered from the effects of the stunning blow he had received. 'Let us conceal ourselves in the cavern and trust the rest to Providence.'

'I remember in having united with two comely maidens in lifting up our voices in praise and thanksgiving,' returned the bewildered singing master, 'since which time I have been visited by a heavy judgement for my sins. I have been mocked by the likeness of sleep, while sounds of discord have rent my ears such as might manifest the fullness of time, and that nature had forgotten her harmony.'

'Poor fellow! Thine own period, was in truth, near its accomplishment. But arouse, and come with me; I will lead you where all other sounds but those of your own psalmody will be excluded.' He led David to the inside of the cavern and concealed the entrance.

'I like not the principle of the natives which teaches them to submit without a struggle in emergencies that appear desperate,' he said while busied in this employment. 'Our own maxim which says, "while life remains there is hope," is more consoling and better suited to a soldier's temperament. To you, Cora, I will urge no words of idle encouragement—your own fortitude and undisturbed reason will teach you all that may become your sex—but cannot we dry the tears of that trembling weeper on your bosom?"'

'I am calmer, Duncan,' said Alice, raising herself from the arms of her sister and forcing an appearance of composure through her tears, 'much calmer now. Surely in this hidden spot we are safe, we are secret, free from injury; we will hope everything from those generous men who have risked so much already in our behalf.'

'Now does our gentle Alice speak like a daughter of Munro!' said Heyward, pausing to press her hand as he passed towards the outer entrance of the cavern. There he seated himself, grasping his remaining pistol with a hand convulsively clenched while his contracted and frowning eyes announced the sullen desperation of his purpose. 'The Hurons, if they come, may not gain our position so easily as they think,' he lowly muttered; and dropping his head back against the rock, he seemed to await the result in patience, though his gaze was unceasingly bent on the open avenue to their place of retreat.

With the last sound of his voice, a deep, a long and almost breathless silence succeeded, that lasted until a sudden yell burst into the air without and caused their hearts to bound into the passage of their throats.

'We are lost!' exclaimed Alice, throwing herself into the arms of Cora.

'Not yet, not yet,' returned the agitated but undaunted Heyward. 'The sound came from the centre of the island, and it has been produced by the sight of their dead companions. We are not yet discovered and there is still hope.'

Faint and almost despairing as was the prospect of escape, the words of Duncan were not thrown away, for it awakened the powers of the sisters in such a manner that they awaited the result in silence. A second yell soon followed the first; then a rush of voices was heard pouring down the island, from its upper to its lower extremity, until they reached the naked rock above the caverns, where, after a shout of savage triumph, the air continued full of horrible cries and screams, such as man alone can utter, and he only in the state of fiercest barbarity.

The sounds quickly spread around them in every direction. Cries were heard in the startling vicinity of the chasm between the two caves, which mingled with the hoarser yells that arose out of the abyss of the deep ravine. In short it was not difficult for the anxious listeners to imagine they could be heard beneath as in truth they were above and on every side of them.

In the midst of this tumult a triumphant yell was raised within a few yards of the hidden entrance to the cave. Heyward abandoned every hope with the belief it was the signal they were discovered. Again the impression passed away as he heard the voices collect near the spot where Hawk-eye had so reluctantly abandoned his rifle. Amid the jargon of the Indian dialogues that he now plainly heard, it was easy to distinguish not only words, but sentences in the patois of the Canadas. A burst of voices had shouted simultaneously, 'La Longue Carabine!' causing the opposite woods to re-echo with a name which, Heyward well remembered, had been given by his enemies to a celebrated hunter and scout of the English camp, and who, he now learned for the first time, had been his late companion whom he knew as Hawk-eye. 'La Longue Carabine! La Longue Carabine!' passed from mouth to mouth until the whole band appeared to be collected around a trophy which would seem to announce the death of its formidable owner and the need to search for his body.

'Now,' Heyward whispered to the trembling sisters, 'now is the moment of uncertainty. If our place of retreat escapes this scrutiny we are still safe. In every event, we are assured by our enemies that our friends have escaped, and that in two short hours we may look for succour from Webb,' Heyward's words of encouragement died on his lips as he caught sight of

Cora's face on which the bloom had given to the paleness of death; her soft melting eyes seemed contracting in horror and her fingers pointed forward in convulsed motion. On the instant he turned his attention from the hidden entrance to the cave from which he was anticipating discovery to the direction in which Cora pointed, and peering just above the ledge which formed the threshold of the open outlet of the cavern, he beheld the malignant, fierce and savage features of Le Renard Subtil.

The look of exultation and brutal triumph which announced this truth was irresistably irritating. Forgetful of everything but the impulses of his hot blood, Duncan levelled his pistol and fired. The report of the weapon made the cavern bellow like an eruption from a volcano, and when the smoke it vomited had been driven away before the current of air which issued from the ravine, the place so lately occupied by the features of his treacherous guide was vacant. Rushing to the outlet, Heyward caught a glimpse of his dark figure stealing around a low and narrow ledge, which soon hid him entirely from sight.

Among the savages a frightful stillness succeeded the explosion which had just been heard bursting from the bowels of the rock. But when Le Renard raised his voice in a long and intelligible whoop, the cavern was entered at both extremities and Duncan and his companions were dragged from their shelter and borne into the day, where they stood surrounded by the whole band of triumphant Hurons. Contrary to the usages of the natives in the wantonness of their success, they had respected, not only the persons of the trembling sisters, but also Duncan's. Emboldened by this, he conquered the disgust he felt in looking at the treacherous face of the one who had so recently acted as his guide and reluctantly addressed Magua.

'Le Renard Subtil is too much of a warrior to refuse telling an unarmed man what his conquerors say.'

'They ask for the hunter who knows the paths through the woods,' returned Magua in his broken

English, laying his hand at the same time, with a ferocious smile, on the bundle of leaves with which a wound on his own shoulder was bandaged. 'La Longue Carabine. The "Long Rifle". His rifle is good and his eye is never shut; but, like the short gun of the white chief, it is nothing against the life of Le Subtil. The red Hurons call for the life of the "Long Rifle", or they will have the blood of him that keep him hid.'

'He is gone—escaped. He is far beyond their reach. Though no fish, the "Long Rifle" can swim. He floated down the stream when the powder was all burnt, and when the eyes of the Hurons were behind a cloud.'

'And why did the white chief stay,' demanded the still incredulous Indian. 'Is he a stone that goes to the bottom, or does the scalp burn his head?'

'I am no stone,' said the provoked young man. 'The white man thinks none but cowards desert their women.'

Magua muttered a few words inaudibly between his teeth, before he continued aloud:

'Can the Delawares swim too, as well as crawl in the bushes? Where is Le Gros Serpent?'

Duncan , who perceived by the use of these Canadian appellations that his late companions were much better known to his enemies than to himself, answered reluctantly: 'If you mean Chingachgook, he also is gone down with the water.'

'Le Cerf Agile is not here?'

'I know not whom you call the "Nimble Deer",' said Duncan, gladly profiting by any excuse to create delay.

'Uncas,' returned Magua, pronouncing the Delaware name with even greater difficulty than he spoke his English words. 'Bounding Elk' is what the white man says when he calls the young Mohican. The deer is swift, the elk is swift but strong, and the son of the Serpent is Le Cerf Agile.'

'If you mean the younger Delaware, he too is gone down with the water.'

As there was nothing improbable to an Indian in the

manner of escape, Magua admitted the truth of what he had heard with a readiness that afforded additional evidence how little he would prize such worthless captives.

When the fact was generally understood, the savages raised a frightful yell which declared the extent of their disappointment in the escape, and Duncan greatly feared for the safety of his little band. His apprehensions, however, were greatly relieved when the leader called the Hurons to a council. By the frequency with which the few speakers pointed in the direction of Webb's encampment, it was apparent they dreaded the approach of danger from that quarter. This consideration probably hastened their determination and quickened their subsequent movement, for they now bore a light bark from the upper end of the rock and placed it in the water near the mouth of the outer cavern. As soon as this change was made, the leader made signs to the prisoners to descend and enter.

As resistance was impossible and remonstrance useless, Heyward set the example of submission by leading the way into the canoe, where he was soon seated with the sisters and still wondering David. The vessel now glided down the current and in a few moments the captives found themselves on the south bank of the stream, nearly opposite to the point where they had struck it the preceding evening.

Here was held another short consultation, during which the horses, to whose panic their owner ascribed their heaviest misfortune, were led from the cover of the woods and brought to the sheltered spot. The band was now divided. The great chief, mounting the charger of Heyward, led the way directly across the river, followed by most of his people, and disappeared in the woods, leaving the prisoners in charge of six savages, at whose head was Le Renard Subtil. Duncan witnessed all their movements with increasing uneasiness.

When all were prepared, Magua made the signal to proceed, advancing in front to lead the party in person. Next followed David, who was gradually coming to a true sense of his condition as the effects of the wounds became less and less apparent. The sisters rode in the rear with Heyward at their side, while the Indians flanked the party and brought up the close of the march with a caution that seemed never to tire.

Cora alone remembered the parting injunctions of the scout, and whenever an opportunity offered she stretched forth her arm to bend aside the twigs that met her hands, though the vigilance of the Indians rendered this act of precaution both difficult and dangerous.

After crossing a low vale, through which a gushing brook meandered, Magua suddenly ascended a hill so steep and difficult that the sisters were compelled to alight in order to follow. When the summit was gained, they found themselves on a level spot, but thinly covered with trees, under one of which Magua flung his dark form, as if willing and ready to seek that rest which was so much needed by the whole party.

While the Indians now gorged themselves on the more preferable parts of a fawn which one of them had found an opportunity to strike down, notwithstanding the swiftness of their flight, he summoned Duncan to him.

'Go', said the Huron. 'Go to the dark-haired maiden and say Magua wishes to speak with her.'

Reluctantly Duncan brought her forward.

'What would Le Renard say to the daughter of Munro,' she asked coldly.

'Listen,' said the Indian, laying his hand firmly upon her arm, 'Magua was born a chief and a warrior among the red Hurons of the lakes; he saw the suns of twenty summers make the snows of twenty winters run off in the streams before he saw a pale-face; and he was happy! Then his Canada fathers came into the woods and taught him to drink the firewater, and he became a rascal. The Hurons drove him from the graves of his fathers as they would chase the hunted buffalo. There he hunted and fished till the people chased him again through the woods into the arms of his enemies.

The chief, who was born a Huron, was at last a warrior among the Mohawks. Was it the fault of Le Renard that his head was not made of rock? Who gave him the firewater?'

'And am I answerable that thoughtless and unprincipled men exist, whose shades of countenance may resemble mine?' demanded Cora.

'Listen' repeated the Indian, resuming his earnest attitude; 'when his English and French fathers dug up the hatchet, Le Renard struck the war-post of the Mohawks and went out against his own nation. The pale-faces have driven the redskins from their hunting grounds and now when they fight, a white man leads the way. The old chief at Horican, your father, was the great captain of our war party. He said to the Mohawks do this, and do that, and he was minded. He made a law that if an Indian swallowed the firewater, and came into the cloth wigwams of his warriors, it should not be forgotten. Magua foolishly opened his mouth, and the hot liquor led him into the cabin of Munro. What did the grey-head? Let his daughter say.'

'He forgot not his words and did justice by punishing the offender,' said the undaunted daughter.

'Justice!' repeated the Indian, casting an oblique glance of the most ferocious expression at her unyielding countenance. 'Magua was not himself; it was the firewater that spoke and acted for him, but Munro did not believe it. The Huron chief was tied up before all the pale-faced warriors and whipped like a dog. When he felt the blows of Munro, his spirit lay under the birch. The spirit of a Huron is never drunk; it remembers for ever!'

'But it may be appeased. If my father has done you this injustice, show him how an Indian can forgive an injury, and take back his daughters.

'Listen!' said the Indian, 'the light-eyes can go back to the Horican, and tell the old chief what has been done, if the dark-haired woman will swear by the Great Spirit of her fathers to follow him and live in his wigwam for ever. When the blows scorched the back of the Huron, he would know where to find a woman to feel the smart. The daughter of Munro would draw his water, hoe his corn and cook his venison. The body of the grey-head would sleep among his cannon, but his heart would lie within reach of the knife of Le Subtil.'

'Monster! Well dost thou deserve thy treacherous name!' cried Cora in an ungovernable burst of filial indignation. 'None but a fiend could meditate such a vengeance. But thou overratest thy power! You shall find it is, in truth, the heart of Munro you hold, and that it will defy your utmost malice!"

The Indian answered this bold defiance with a ghastly smile that showed an unaltered purpose, while he motioned her away as if to close the conference for ever. Cora, already regretting her precipitation, was obliged to comply, for Magua instantly left the spot, and approached his gluttonous comrades. Heyward flew to the side of the agitated female, and demanded the result of a dialogue that he had watched at a distance with so much interest. But, unwilling to alarm the fears of Alice, she evaded a direct reply. Her choked utterance, however, spoke more impressively than any words, and quickly drew the attention of her companions to Magua on whom her own eyes were riveted with an intentness that nothing but the importance of the stake could create. He having now reached the cluster of lolling savages who, gorged with their disgusting meal, lay stretched on the earth in brutal indulgence, had now commenced speaking with the dignity of an Indian chief. The first syllables he uttered had the effect to cause his listeners to raise themselves in attitudes of respectful attention, and although the listeners understood nothing of what was said, they realized he was working them up to a frenzy of rage, using every artifice known to an orator. At last, when he had lifted his voice to a pitch of terrific energy, his words ended in a burst of rage which now broke into the air, as if the wood, instead of containing so small a band, was filled with the nation.

The whole band sprang upon their feet as one man; giving utterance to their rage in the most frantic cries, they rushed upon the prisoners with drawn knives and uplifted tomahawks. Heyward threw himself between the sisters and the foremost, whom he grappled with a desperate strength that for a moment checked his violence. This unexpected resistance gave Magua time to interpose, and with rapid enunciation and animated gestures he drew the attention of the band again to himself. In that language he knew so well how to assume, he diverted his comrades from their instant purpose, and invited them to prolong the misery of their victims. His proposal was received with acclamations, and executed with the swiftness of thought.

Two powerful warriors cast themselves on Heyward, while another was occupied in securing the less active singing master. Neither of the captives, however, submitted without a desperate, though fruitless struggle Even David hurled his assailant to the earth; nor was Heyward secured until the victory over his companion enabled the Indians to direct their united force to that object; he was then bound and fastened to the body of a sapling. On his right was Cora, in a durance similar to his own, pale and agitated, but with an eye whose steady look still read the proceedings of their enemies. On his left, the withes which bound her to a pine performed that office for Alice which her trembling limbs refused, and alone kept her fragile form from sinking.

The vengeance of the Hurons now became clear. Some sought knots to raise a blazing pile; others, splinters of pine that would pierce the flesh of their captives with the burning fragments. But the vengeance of Magua now sought a deeper and more malignant enjoyment.

'Ha!' he jeered, approaching Cora, 'What says the daughter of Munro? Her head is too good to find a pillow in the wigwam of Le Renard; will she like it better when it rolls about this hill a plaything for the wolves? Her bosom cannot nurse the children of a Huron; she will see it spit upon by Indians.'

'What means the monster?' demanded the astonished Heyward.

'Nothing,' was the firm reply. 'He is a savage—a barbarous and ignorant savage—and knows what he does.'

'Say', cried the fierce Huron, 'shall I send the yellow-hair to her father, and will you follow Magua to the great lakes, to carry water, and feed him with corn?'

Cora beckoned him away, with an emotion of disgust she could not control.

'Leave me,' she said with a solemnity that for a moment checked the barbarity of the Indian; 'you mingle bitterness in my prayers; you stand between me and my God.'

For many moments the elder sister looked upon the younger with a countenance that wavered with powerful and contending emotions. At length she spoke, though her tones had lost their rich, calm fullness in an expression of tenderness that seemed maternal.

'Alice,' she said, 'the Huron offers us both life—nay more than both; he offers to restore Duncan—our invaluable Duncan, as well as you, to our friends—to our father—to our heart-stricken, childless father, if I will bow down this rebellious stubborn pride of mine, and consent... to become his wife. Speak then, Alice, child of my affections, sister of my love. And you too, Major Heyward, aid my weak reason with your counsel. Is life to be purchased by such a sacrifice? Will you, Alice, receive it at my hands at such a price? And you, Duncan, guide me; control me between you, for I am wholly yours.'

'Would I?' echoed the indignant and astonished youth. 'Cora, Cora, you jest with our misery! Name the horrid alternative again; the thought itself is worse than a thousand deaths!'

'That such would be your answer I well knew!' exclaimed Cora, her cheeks flushing, and her dark eyes once more sparkling with the lingering emotions of a woman. 'What says my Alice? For her will I submit without another murmur.'

'No, no, no!' came the reply. 'Better that we die, as we have lived, together!'

'Then die!' shouted Magua, hurling his tomahawk with violence at the unresisting speaker, and gnashing his teeth with a rage that could no longer be bridled at this sudden exhibition of firmness in one he believed to be the weakest in the party. The axe cleaved the air in front of Heyward, and, cutting some of the flowing ringlets of Alice, quivered in the tree above her head. The sight maddened Duncan to desperation. Collecting all his energies in one effort, he snapped the twigs that bound him and rushed upon another savage, who was preparing with loud yells, and a more deliberate aim, to repeat the blow. They encountered, grappled and fell to the earth together. The naked body of his antagonist afforded Heyward no means of holding his adversary, who glided from his grasp and rose again with one knee on his chest, pressing him down with the weight of a giant. Duncan already saw the knife gleaming in the air, when a whistling sound swept past him, and was rather accompanied than followed by the sharp crack of a rifle. He felt his breast relieved from the load it had endured ; he saw the savage expression on his adversary's countenance change to a look of vacant wildness, when the Indian fell dead on the faded leaves by his side.

5

THE SISTERS FIND THEIR FATHER

The Hurons stood aghast at this sudden visitation
of death on one of their band, and the names of 'La
Longue Carabine', 'Le Cerf Agile', 'Le Gros Serpent'
burst simultaneously from every lip, and was succeeded by a wild and a sort of plaintive howl. The cry was
answered by a shout from a little thicket, where the
incautious party had piled their arms, and at the next
moment, Hawk-eye, too eager to load the rifle he had
regained, was seen advancing upon them, brandishing
a clubbed weapon, and cutting the air with wide and
powerful sweeps. Bold and rapid as was the progress
of the scout, it was exceeded by that of a light and
vigorous form which, bounding past him, leapt with
incredible activity and daring into the very centre of
the Hurons, where it stood, whirling a tomahawk and
flourishing a glittering knife with fearful menaces, in
front of Cora. Quicker than the thoughts could follow
these unexpected and audacious movements, an image,
armed in the enigmatic panoply of death, glided before
their eyes and assumed a threatening attitude at the
other's side. The savage tormentors recoiled before
these warlike intruders, but the wary and vigilant
leader of the Hurons was not so easily disconcerted.
Casting his keen eyes around the little plain, he rushed
with a loud whoop on the expecting Chingachgook.
It was the signal for a general combat. Neither party
had firearms and the contest was to be decided in the
deadliest manner—hand-to-hand with weapons of offence and none of defence. One by one the Hurons fell
before the dreaded onslaught, and one who was unwise

enough to attack Cora was slain by the joint blows of
Heyward and Hawk-eye and the knife of Uncas.

The battle was now entirely terminated with the
exception of the protracted struggle between 'Le Renard
Subtil' and 'Le Gros Serpent'. The others were unable
to help as the two combatants moved so quickly. Their
swift evolutions seemed to incorporate their bodies
into one, and a blow aimed at one might well have landed on the other. In this manner the two deadly foes
removed in grim combat from the centre of the plain to
its verge. Here at last the Mohican found an opportunity to make a powerful thrust with his knife; Magua
suddenly relinquished his grasp and fell backward
without motion, and seemingly without life. His adversary leapt on his feet, making the arches of the forest
ring with the sounds of triumph.

'Well done for the Delawares! Victory to the Mohican!' cried Hawk-eye, once more elevating the butt of
the long and fatal rifle. 'A finishing blow from a man
without a cross will never tell against his honour, nor
rob him of his right to the scalp!'

But at the very moment when the dangerous weapon
was descending, the subtle Huron rolled swiftly from
beneath the danger, over the edge of the precipice, and
falling on his feet below was seen leaping with a single
bound into the centre of a thicket of low bushes which
clung along its sides. The Delawares, who had believed
their enemy dead, uttered their exclamation of surprise,
and were following with speed and clamour, like hounds
in open view of the deer, when a shrill and peculiar cry
from the scout instantly changed their purpose and
recalled them to the summit of the hill. Hawk-eye now
went round the corpses and thrust his knife into their
bosoms to ensure that they were really dead, but Uncas
flew, with instinctive delicacy, accompanied by Heyward, to the assistance of the females, and quickly
releasing them, placed Alice in the arms of Cora. Their
thanksgivings were dry and silent and utterly beyond
speech. David on the other hand, when released by
Hawk-eye after enduring his suffering with most

exemplary patience, expressed his thanks to providence by producing his book, putting on his spectacles and singing a song of praise to the tune 'Northampton'. The scout meanwhile walked away to collect and to examine into the state of the captured arsenal of the Hurons. In this office he was now joined by Chingachgook, who found his own, as well as the rifle of his son, among the arms. Even Heyward and David were furnished with weapons; nor was ammunition wanting to render them all effectual.

When the foresters had made their selection and distributed their prizes, the scout announced that the hour had arrived when it was necessary to move. Aided by Duncan and the younger Mohican, the sisters descended the sides of the hill which they had so lately ascended under so very different auspices, and whose summit had so nearly proved the scene of their massacre. At the foot they found their Narraganset horses browsing the herbage of the bushes, and, having mounted, they followed the movements of a guide who, in the most deadly straits, has so often proved himself their friend. The journey was, however, short. Hawk-eye leaving the blind path that the Hurons had followed, turned short to his right, and entering the thicket, he crossed a babbling brook and halted in a narrow dell under the shade of a few water-elms. Their distance from the base of the fatal hill was but a few rods and the steeds had been serviceable only in crossing the shallow stream.

The scout and the Indians appeared to be familiar with the sequestered place where they now were, for leaning their rifles against the trees, they commenced throwing aside the dried leaves and opening the blue clay, out of which a clear and sparkling spring of bright, glancing water quickly bubbled. The white man looked about him, as though seeking for some object which was not to be found as readily as he expected.

'These careless imps, the Mohawks, have been here slaking their thirst,' he muttered, 'and the vagabonds have thrown away the gourd.'

Uncas silently extended towards him the desired gourd which he had detected on the branch of an elm and Hawk-eye took a long drink and coolly seated himself.

Heyward, perceiving that their guides now set about their repast in sober earnest, assisted the ladies to alight and placed himself at their side, not unwilling to enjoy a few moments of grateful rest after the bloody scene he had just gone through. While the culinary process was in hand, curiosity induced him to inquire into the circumstances which had led to their timely and unexpected rescue.

'How is that we see you so soon, my generous friend,' he asked, 'and without aid from the garrison of Fort Edward?'

'Had we gone to the bend in the river we might have been in time to rake the leaves over your bodies, but too late to have saved your scalps,' coolly answered the scout. 'No, we lay by under the bank of the Hudson, waiting to watch the movements of the Hurons.'

'You were then witness of all that passed?

'Not of all, for Indian sight is too keen to be easily cheated and we kept close. A difficult matter it was too, to keep this Mohican boy snug in the ambushment.'

'You saw our capture?' Heyward next demanded.

'We heard it,' was the significant answer. 'An Indian yell is plain language to men who have passed their days in the woods. But when you landed we were driven to crawl like serpents beneath the leaves and then we lost sight of you entirely until we placed eyes on you again, trussed to the trees and ready bound for an Indian massacre.'

'Our rescue was the deed of Providence. It was nearly a miracle that you did not mistake the path, for the Hurons divided and each band had its horses.'

'Ay, there we were thrown off the scent, and might indeed have lost the trail had it not been for Uncas. He was bold enough to say that the beasts ridden by the gentle ones,' continued Hawk-eye, glancing his eyes, not without curiosity, on the fillies of the ladies, 'planted the legs of one side on the ground at the same time, which is contrary to the movements of all trotting four-footed animals of my knowledge except the bear. And yet here are horses that always journey in this manner, as my own eyes have seen, and their trail has shown for twenty long miles.'

"'Tis the merit of the animal. They come from the shores of Narraganset Bay, in the small province of Providence Plantations, and are celebrated for their hardiness and the ease of this peculiar movement, though other horses are not unfrequently trained to the same.'

'It may be, it may be,' said Hawk-eye, who had listened with singular attention to this explanation. 'Though I am a man who has the full blood of the whites, my judgement in deer and beaver is greater than in beasts of burden. Uncas had seen their movement and their trail led us on till it struck me the Mingoes would push for this spring, for the knaves know well the virtue of its waters.'

'Is it then so famous?' demanded Heyward, examining with a more curious eye the secluded dell with its bubbling fountain, surrounded as it was with earth of a deep, dingy brown.

'Few redskins who travel south and east of the great lakes but have heard of its qualities. Will you taste for yourself?'

Heyward took the gourd, and after swallowing a little of the water, threw it aside with grimaces of discontent. The scout laughed in his silent but heartfelt manner and shook his head with vast satisfaction.

'Ah! You want the flavour that one gets by habit; time was when I liked it as little as yourself; but I have come to my taste, and now I crave it as a deer does the salt licks. Your high-spiced wines are not better liked than a redskin relishes this water, especially when his nature is failing. But come, Uncas has made his fire and it is time we think of eating, for our journey is long and all before us.'

Interrupting the dialogue by this abrupt transition, the scout had instant recourse to the fragments of food which had escaped the voracity of the Hurons.

When this necessary, but grateful duty had been performed, each of the foresters stooped and took a long parting draught of the solitary and silent spring. Then Hawk-eye announced his determination to proceed. The sisters resumed their saddles, Duncan and David grasped their rifles and followed on their footsteps; the scout leading the advance and the Mohicans bringing up the rear. The whole party moved swiftly through the narrow path towards the north.

The route taken by Hawk-eye lay across those sandy plains, relieved by occasional valleys and swells of land, which had been traversed by their party on the morning of the same day with the baffled Magua for their guide. The sun had now fallen low towards the distant mountains, and, as their journey lay through the interminable forest, the heat was no longer oppressive. Their progress, in consequence, was proportionate, and long before the twilight gathered about them they had made good many toilsome miles on their return.

When the sun neared the horizon in a flood of golden glory, Hawk-eye turned suddenly and pointing upwards towards the gorgeous heavens, began to speak:

'Yonder is the signal given to man to seek his food and natural rest,' he said. 'Our night, however, will soon be over, for with the moon, we must be up and moving again. I remember to have fought the Maquas hereaways, in the first war in which I ever drew blood from a man; and we threw up a work of blocks to keep the ravenous varments from handling our scalps. If my marks do not fail me we shall find the place a few rods farther to our left.'

Without waiting for an assent, or indeed for any reply, the sturdy hunter moved boldly into a dense thicket of young chestnuts. After penetrating through the brush, matted as it was with briars, for a few hundred feet, he entered an open space that surrounded a low green hillock which was crowned by the decayed block-house in question. This rude and neglected building was one of those deserted works which, having been thrown up on an emergency, had been abandoned with the disappearance of danger, and was now quietly crumbling in the solitude of the forest, neglected and nearly forgotten, like the circumstances which had caused it to be reared.

While Heyward and his companions hesitated to approach a building so decayed, Hawk-eye and the Indians entered within the low walls, not only without fear but with obvious interest. While the former surveyed the ruins, both internally and externally, with the curiosity of one whose recollections were reviving at each moment, Chingachgook related to his son, in the language of the Delawares and with the pride of a conqueror, the brief history of the skirmish which had been fought on his youth in that secluded spot. In the meantime, the sisters gladly dismounted and prepared to enjoy their halt in the coolness of the evening and in a security which they believed nothing but the beasts of the forest could invade.

'Would not our resting-place have been more retired, my worthy friend,' demanded the more vigilant Duncan, perceiving that the scout had already finished his short survey, 'had we chosen a spot less known, and one more rarely visited than this?'

'Few live who know the block-house was ever raised,' was the slow and musing answer. ''Tis not often that books are made and narratives written of such a scrimmage as was here fought atween the Mohicans and the Mohawks in a war of their own waging. I was then a younker and went out with the Delawares because I know'd they were a scandalized and wronged race. Forty days and forty nights did the imps' crave our blood around this pile of logs, which I designed and partly reared, being, as you'll remember, no Indian myself, but a man without a cross. The Delawares lent themselves to the work, and we made it good, and then we sallied out upon the hounds and not a man of them ever got back to tell the fate of his party. Yes, yes,

I was young then, and new to the sight of blood; and not relishing the thought that creatures who had spirits like myself should lay on the naked ground, to be torn asunder by beasts, or to bleach in the rains, I buried the dead with my own hands under that very little hillock where you have placed yourselves; and no bad seat does it make, neither, though it be raised by the bones of mortal men.'

Heyward and the sisters arose on the instant from the grassy sepulchre of the dead Mohawks. Hawk-eye waved them back.

'They are gone, and they are harmless,' he continued. 'They'll never shout the war-whoop again. And of all those who aided in placing them where they lie, Chingachgook and I alone are living. You see before you all that are now left of his race,'

The hunter and his companions now busied themselves in preparations for the comfort and protection of those they guided. A spring, which many long years before had induced the natives to select a place for their temporary fortification, was soon cleared of leaves and a fountain of crystal gushed from the bed, diffusing its waters over the verdant hillock. A corner of the building was then roofed in such a manner as to exclude the heavy dew of the climate, and piles of sweet shrubs and dried leaves were laid beneath if for the sisters to repose on.

While the diligent woodsmen were employed in this manner, Cora and Alice partook of that refreshment which duty required much more than inclination prompted them to accept.

Duncan had prepared himself to pass the night in watchfulness near them, just without the ruin, but the scout, perceiving his intentions, pointed towards Chingachgook as he coolly disposed his own person on the grass, and said:

'The eyes of a white man are too heavy and blind for such a watch as this. The Mohican will be our sentinel, therefore let us sleep, and sleep in safety.'

The tired Duncan yielded to persuasion and how long he lay in this insensible state he never knew himself, but his slumbering visions had not long been lost in total forgetfulness when he was awakened by a light tap on the shoulder. Aroused by this signal, slight as it was, he sprang upon his feet with a confused recollection of the self-imposed duty he had assumed with the commencement of the night:

'Who comes?' he demanded, feeling for his sword at the place where it was usually suspended. 'Speak! Friend or enemy?'

'Friend,' replied the low voice of Chingachgook, who, pointing upwards at the luminary which was shedding its mild light through the opening in the trees directly on their bivouac, immediately added in his rude English: 'Moon comes—and white man's fort far-far off; time to move when sleep shuts both eyes of the Frenchmen!'

'You say true! Call up our friends and bridle the horses, while I prepare my own companions for the march!'

'We are awake, Duncan,' said the soft, silvery tones of Alice within the building, 'and ready to travel very fast after so refreshing a sleep.'

'Hush! The Mohicans hear an enemy!' whispered Hawk-eye, who by this time, in common with the whole party, was awake and stirring. 'They scent danger in the wind! Lead the horses into the block-house, Uncas; and friends, do you follow to the same shelter. Poor and old as it is, it offers a cover, and has rung with the crack of a rifle afore tonight.'

He was instantly obeyed, the Mohicans leading the Narragansets within the ruin, whither the whole party repaired with the most guarded silence.

The sounds of approaching footsteps were now too distinctly audible to leave any doubts as to the nature of the interruption. They were soon mingled with voices calling to each other in an Indian dialect, which the hunter, in a whisper, affirmed to Heyward was the language of the Hurons. When the party reached the point where the horses had entered the thicket which surrounded the block-house, they were evidently at fault, having lost those marks which, until that moment, had directed their pursuit.

It would seem by the voices that twenty men were soon collected at that one spot, mingling their different opinions and advice in noisy clamour.

'The knaves know our weakness,' whispered Hawkeye, who stood by the side of Heyward in deep shade, looking through an opening in the logs, 'or they wouldn't indulge their idleness in such a squaws' march. Listen to the reptiles, each man among them seems to have two tongues and but a single leg !'

The search of the savages proved fruitless; for so short and sudden had been the passage from the faint path the travellers had journeyed into the thicket, that every trace of their footsteps was lost in the obscurity of the woods.

It was not long, however, before the restless savages were heard beating the brush, and gradually approaching the inner circle of that dense border of young chestnuts which surrounded the little area.

A moment later the thicket opened and a tall and armed Huron advanced a few paces into the open space. As he gazed upon the silent block-house, the moon fell upon his swarthy countenance and betrayed its surprise and curiosity. He made the exclamation which usually accompanies the former emotion in an Indian, and calling in a low voice soon drew a companion to his side. With slow and cautious steps they approached, pausing every instant to look at the building until the foot of one of them suddenly rested on the mound, and he stooped to examine its nature.

The savages were now so near that the last emotion in one of the horses, or even a breath louder than common would have betrayed the fugitives. But in discovering the character of the mound, the attention of the Hurons appeared directed to a different object. Then they drew warily back, keeping their eyes riveted on the ruin, as if they expected to see the apparitions of the dead issue from its silent walls, until having reached the boundary of the area, they moved slowly into the thicket and disappeared.

Hawk-eye dropped the breech of his rifle to the earth, and drawing a long, free breath, exclaimed in an audible whisper:

'Ay! They respect the dead, and it has this time saved their own lives and maybe, the lives of better men too.'

Hawk-eye waited until a signal from the listening Chingachgook assured him that every sound from the retiring party was completely swallowed by the distance, when he motioned to Heyward to lead forth the horses and to assist the sisters into their saddles. The instant this was done they issued through the broken gateway, and stealing out by a direction opposite to the one by which they had entered, they quitted the spot, the sisters casting furtive glances at the silent grave and crumbling ruin as they left the soft light of the moon to bury themselves in the gloom of the woods.

During the rapid movement from the block-house, and until the party was deeply buried in the forest, each individual was too much interested in the escape to hazard a word even in whispers. But when the banks of a little stream were gained, Hawk-eye made another halt; and taking the moccasins from his feet he invited Heyward and Gamut to follow his example. He then entered the water and for near an hour they travelled in the bed of the brook, leaving no trail. The moon had already sunk into an immense pile of black clouds, which lay impending above the western horizon,. when they issued from the low and devious watercourse to rise again to the light and level of the sandy but wooded plain. Here the scout seemed to be once more at home, for he held on his way with the certainty and diligence of a man who moved in the security of his own knowledge. The path soon became more uneven and the travellers could plainly perceive that the mountains drew nigher to them on each hand, and that they were, in truth, about entering one of their gorges. Suddenly Hawk-eye made a pause, and waiting until he was joined by the whole party, he spoke, though in tones so low and cautious that they added to the solemnity of his words in the quiet and darkness of the place.

'It is easy to know the pathways and to find the licks and watercourses of the wilderness,' he said, 'but who that saw this spot could venture to say that a mighty army was at rest among yonder silent trees and barren mountains?'

'We are then, at no great distance from William Henry?' said Heyward, advancing nigher to the scout.

'It is yet a long and weary path, and when and where to strike it, is now our greatest difficulty. By heaven! There is a human form, and it approaches! Stand to your arms, my friends, for we know not whom we encounter.'

'Qui vive?' demanded a stern, quick voice, which sounded like a challenge from another world, issuing out of that solitary and solmen place.

'What says it?' demanded the scout. 'It speaks neither English nor Indian!'

'Qui vive?' repeated the same voice, which was quickly followed by the rattling of arms, and a menacing attitude.

'France' cried Heyward, advancing from the shadow of the trees to the shore of the pond, within a few yards of the sentinel.

'D'ou venez-vous — où allez-vous, d'aussi bonne heure?' demanded the grenadier, in the language and the accent of a man from old France.

'Je viens de la découverte, et je vais me coucher.'

'Êtes-vous officier du roi?'

'Sans doute, mon camarade; me prends-tu pour un provencial! Je suis captaine de chasseurs' (Heyward well knew that the other was a regiment of the line); j'ai ici avec moi les filles du commandant de la fortification. Aha! Tu en as entendu parler! Je les ai fait prisonnières près de l'autre fort, et je les conduis au général.'

'Ma foi, mesdames! J'en suis faché pour vous,' exclaimed the young soldier, touching his cap with grace; 'mais—fortune de guerre! Vous trouverez notre général un brave homme, et bien poli avec les dames.'

'C'est le caractère des gens de guerre,' said Cora with admirable self-possession. 'Adieu, mon ami; je vous souhaiterais un devoir plus agréable à remplir.'

The soldier made a low and humble acknowledgement for her civility; and Heyward adding a 'bonne nuit, mon camarade,' they moved deliberately forward leaving the sentinel pacing the banks of the silent pond, little suspecting an enemy of so much effrontery and humming to himself those words, which were recalled to his mind by the sight of women, and perhaps by recollections of his own distant and beautiful France:

'Vive le vin, vive l'amour,' etc., etc.,

'Tis well you understood the knave,' whispered the scout when they had gained a little distance from the place, and letting his rifle fall into the hollow of his arm again. 'I soon saw that he was one of them uneasy Frenchers; and well for him it was, that his speech was friendly, and his wishes kind, or a place might have been found for his bones amongst those of his countrymen.'

He was interrupted by a long and heavy groan which arose from the little basin, as though, in truth, the spirits of the departed lingered about their watery sepulchre.

. 'Surely it was of flesh,' continued the scout; 'no spirit could handle its arms so steadily.'

'It was of flesh, but whether the poor fellow still belongs to this world may well be doubted,' said Heyward glancing his eyes around him, and missing Chingachgook from their little band. Then the form of the Indian was seen gliding out of the thicket. As the chief rejoined them, with one hand he attached the reeking scalp of the unfortunate young Frenchman to his girdle and with the other he replaced the knife and tomahawk that had drunk his blood. He then took his wonted station with the air of a man who believed he had done a deed of merit.

The scout stood musing in profound silence.

"Tis the gift and nature of an Indian, and, though better it were left undone, cannot be amended. You see we are too obviously within the sentinels of the enemy the French have gathered round the fort in good earnest. We must turn on our tail and get without the line of their lookouts; then we will bend short to the west and enter the mountains where I can hide you so that all the devil's hounds in Montcalm's pay would be thrown off the scent for months to come.'

'Let it be done, and that instantly!'

Further words were unnecessary, for Hawk-eye, merely uttering the mandate 'to follow' moved along the route by which they had just entered their present critical and even dangerous situation. Their progress, like their late dialogue, was guarded and without noise; for none knew at what moment a passing patrol, or a crouching picket of the enemy might rise upon their path.

Hawk-eye soon deviated from the line of their retreat and striking off towards the mountains that form the western boundary of the narrow plain, he led his followers, with swift steps, deep within the shadows that were cast from their high and broken summits. The route was now painful, lying over ground ragged with rocks and intersected with ravines, and their progress proportionately slow. Bleak and black hills lay on every side of them compensating in some degree for the additional toil of the march by the sense of security they imparted. At length the party began slowly to rise a steep and rugged ascent, by a path that curiously wound among rocks and trees, avoiding the one and supported by the other, in a manner that showed it had been devised by men long practised in the arts of the wilderness. When they issued from the stunted woods that clung to the barren sides of the mountains, upon a flat and mossy rock that formed its summit, they met the morning as it came blushing among the green pines of a hill that lay on the opposite side of the valley of the Horican.

The scout now told the sisters to dismount; and taking the bridles from the mouths, and the saddles off the backs of the jaded beasts, he turned them loose to glean a scanty subsidence amongst the shrubs and meagre herbage of that elevated region.

'Go,' he said, 'and seek your food where nature gives it you; and beware you become not food to ravenous wolves yourselves among these hills. We have too much need now for caution and silence to have further need of you.'

Pushing on on foot the travellers reached the verge of the precipice ahead of them and saw at a glance the truth of the scout's declaration, and the admirable foresight with which he'd led them to their commanding station.

The mountain on which they stood, elevated, perhaps, a thousand feet in the air, was a high cone that rose a little in advance of that range which stretches for miles along the western shores of the lake, until, meeting its sister piles upon the water, it ran off towards the Canadas in confused and broken masses of rock thinly sprinkled with evergreens. Immediately at the feet of the party the southern shore of the Horican swept in a broad semicircle, from mountain to mountain, marking a wide strand that soon rose to an uneven and somewhat elevated plain. To the north stretched the limpid, and as it appeared from that dizzy height, the narrow sheet of the Holy Lake, indented with numberless bays, embellished by fantastic headlands, and dotted with countless islands. At a distance of a few leagues the bed of the waters became lost among mountains, or was wrapped in masses of vapour that came slowly rolling along their bosom before a light morning air. But a narrow opening between the crests of the hills pointed out the passage by which they found their way still farther north, to spread their pure and ample sheets again before pouring out their tribute into the distant Champlain. To the south stretched the defile, or rather broken plain, so often mentioned. For several miles in this direction the mountains appeared reluctant to yield their dominion, but within reach of the eye they diverged, and finally melted into the level and sandy lands across which we have accompanied our adventurers in their double journey. Along both ranges of hills which bounded the opposite sides of the lake and valley, clouds of light vapour were rising in spiral wreaths from the uninhabited woods, looking like the smokes of hidden cottages, or rolled lazily down the declivities to mingle with the fogs of the lower land. A single, solitary, snow-white cloud floated above the valley and marked the sport beneath which lay the silent pool of the 'bloody pond.'

Directly on the shore of the lake, and nearer to its western than its eastern margin, lay the extensive earthen ramparts and low buildings of William Henry. Two of the sweeping bastions appeared to rest on the water which washed their bases, while a deep ditch and extensive morasses guarded its other sides and angles. The land had been cleared for wood for a reasonable distance around the work, but every other part of the scene lay in the green livery of nature, except where the limpid water mellowed the view, or the rocks thrust their naked heads above the undulating ranges of the mountain ranges. In its front might be seen the scattered sentinels, who held a weary watch against their numerous foes; and within the walls themselves the travellers looked down upon men still drowsy with a night of vigilance. Towards the south-east, but in immediate contact with the fort, was an entrenched camp, posted on a rocky eminence that would have been far more eligible for the the work itself, in which Hawkeye pointed out the presence of those auxiliary regiments that had so recently left the Hudson in their company. From the woods, a little farther to the south, rose numerous dark and lurid smokes, that were easily to be distinguished from the purer exhalations of the springs, and which the scout also showed to Heyward as evidence that the enemy lay in force in that direction.

But the spectacle that most concerned the young soldier was on the western bank of the lake, though quite near to its southern termination. On a strip of land, which appeared from his stand too narrow to contain such an army, but which in truth extended many hundreds of yards from the shores of the Horican to the base of the mountain, were to be seen the white tents and military engines of an encampment of ten thousand men. Batteries were already thrown up in their front, and even while the spectators above them were looking down with such different emotions on a scene which lay like a map beneath their feet, the roar of artillery rose from the valley, and passed off in thundering echoes along the eastern hills.

'Morning is just touching them below,' said the deliberate and musing scout, 'and the watchers have a mind to wake up the sleepers by the sound of cannon. We are a few hours too late. Montcalm has already filled the woods with his accursed Iroquois.

'Ha! Here will soon be an end of the firing for yonder comes a fog that will turn day to night, and make an Indian arrow more dangerous than a moulded cannon. Now, if you are equal to the work and will follow, I will make a push; for I long to get down into that camp, if it be only to scatter some Mingo dogs that I see lurking in the skirts of yonder thicket of birch.'

'We are equal' said Cora firmly; 'on such an errand we will follow to any danger.'

The scout turned to her with a smile of honest and cordial approbation as he answered:

'I would I had a thousand men, of brawny limbs and quick eyes, that feared death as little as you! But the fog comes rolling down so fast, we shall have but just the time to meet it on the plain, and use it as cover. Remember if any accident should befall me, to keep the air blowing on your left cheeks, or, rather follow the Mohicans; they'd scent their way, be it day or night.'

He then waved his hand for them to follow, and threw himself down the deep declivity with free but careful footsteps. Heyward helped the sisters to descend and in a few minutes they were all down a mountain whose sides they had climbed with so much toil and pain.

The direction taken by Hawk-eye soon brought the travellers to the level of the plain, nearly opposite to a sally-port in the western curtain of the fort, which lay itself at a distance of about half-a-mile from the point where he halted to allow Duncan to come up with his charge. In their eagerness, and favoured by the nature of the ground, they had anticipated the fog which was rolling down the lake, and it became necessary to pause until the mists had wrapped the camp of the enemy in their fleecy mantle. The scout and the Mohicans profited by the delay to steal out of the woods, and to make a survey of surrounding objects.

In a very few moments they returned, the scout's face reddened with vexation, while he muttered his words of disappointment in words of no very gentle import.

'Here has the cunning Frenchman been posting a picket directly in our path,' he said, 'redskins and whites and we shall be as likely to fall into their midst as to pass them in the fog.'

He was yet speaking when a crashing sound was heard, and a cannon-ball entered the thicket, striking the body of a sapling and rebounding to the earth its force being very much expended by the previous resistance.

'This shot that you see,' said the scout, kicking the harmless iron with his foot, 'has ploughed the earth from the fort, and we shall hunt for the furrow it has made when all other signs fail. No more words but follow or the fog may leave us in the middle of our path, a mark for both armies to shoot at.'

They had, as Heyward thought, got over nearly half the distance to the friendly works, when his ears were saluted with the fierce summons:

'Qui va là?'

'Push on,' whispered the scout, once more bending to the left.

'Push on,' repeated Heyward, when the summons was renewed by a dozen voices, each of which seemed charged with menace.

'C'est moi,' cried Duncan, dragging rather than leading those he supported swiftly forward.

'Bête! Qui? Moi!'

'Ami de la France.'

'Tu m'as plus l'air d'un ennemi de la France. Arrête, ou pardieu je te ferai ami du diable. Feu! Camarades, feu!'

The order was instantly obeyed, and the fog was stirred by the explosion of fifty muskets. Happily the aim was bad and the bullets cut the air in a direction a little different from that taken by the fugitives, though still so nigh that to the unpractised ears of David and the two females it appeared as if they whistled within a few inches of the organs. The outcry was renewed and the order, not only to fire again, but to pursue, was but too plainly audible. When Heyward briefly explained the meaning of the words they heard, Hawk-eye halted, and spoke with quick decision and great firmness.

'Let us deliver our fire,' he said; 'they will believe it is a sortie, and give way, or they will wait for reinforcements.'

The scheme was well conceived but failed in its effect. The instant the French heard the pieces it seemed as if the plain was alive with men, muskets rattling along its whole extent, from the shores of the lake to the farthest boundary of the woods.

'We shall draw their entire army upon us, and bring on a general assault,' said Duncan. 'Lead on, my friend, for your own life and ours.'

The scout seemed willing to comply but in the hurry of the moment he had lost the direction. In this dilemma Uncas lighted on the furrow of the cannon-ball, where it had cut the ground in three adjacent ant-hills.

'Give me the range!' said Hawk-eye, bending to catch a glimpse of the direction and then instantly moving onward.

Cries, oaths, voices calling to each other, and the reports of muskets, were now quick and incessant, and, apparently on every side of them. Suddenly a strong glare of light flashed across the scene, the fog rolled upwards in thick wreaths, and several cannons belched across the plain, and the roar was thrown heavily back from the bellowing echoes of the mountain.

"Tis from the fort!' exclaimed Hawk-eye, turning short on his tracks; 'and we, like stricken fools, were rushing to the woods under the very knives of the Maquas.'

The instant their mistake was rectified, the whole party retraced the error with the utmost diligence. Duncan willingly relinquished the support of Cora to the arms of Uncas, and Cora as readily accepted the welcome assistance. Men, hot and angry in pursuit, were evidently on their footsteps, and each instant threatened their capture, if not their destruction.

'Point de quartier aux coquins!' cried an eager pursuer, who seemed to direct the operations of the enemy.

'Stand firm and be ready, my gallant 60ths!' suddenly exclaimed a voice above them. 'Wait to see the enemy; fire low and sweep the glacis.'

'Father! Father!' exclaimed a piercing cry from out of the mist. 'It is I, Alice, thine own Elsie! Spare, oh, save your daughters!'

'Hold!' shouted the former speaker in the awful tones of parental agony, the sound reaching even to the woods and rolling back in solemn echo. "Tis she! God has restored me my children! Throw open the sally-port! To the field, 60ths, to the field! Pull not a trigger lest ye kill my lambs! Drive off these dogs of France with your steel!'

Duncan heard the grating of the rusty hinges, and, darting to the spot directed by the sound, he met a long line of dark red warriors passing swiftly towards the glacis. He knew them for his own battalion of the royal Americans, and, flying to their head, soon swept every trace of his pursuers from before the works.

For an instant Cora and Alice had stood trembling and bewildered by the unexpected desertion, but before either had leisure for speech, or even thought, an officer of gigantic frame, whose locks were bleached with years and service, but whose air of military grandeur had been rather softened than destroyed by time, rushed out of the body of the mist and folded them to his bosom, while large scalding tears rolled down his pale and wrinkled cheeks, and he exclaimed in the accent of Scotland:

'For this I thank thee, Lord! Let danger come as it will. Thy servant is now prepared!'

6

DEFEAT AND TREACHERY

A few succeeding days were passed amid the privations, the uproar and the dangers of the siege, which
was vigorously pressed by a power against whose approaches Munro possessed no competent means of
resistance. It appeared as if Webb, with his army,
which lay slumbering on the banks of the Hudson,
had utterly forgotten the strait to which his countrymen were reduced. Montcalm had filled the woods of
the portage with his savages, every yell and whoop from
whom rang through the British encampment, chilling
the hearts of men who were already but too much disposed to magnify the danger.

It was in the afternoon of the fifth day of the siege,
and the fourth of his own service in it, that Major Heyward profited by a parley that had just been beaten, by
repairing to the ramparts of one of the water bastions
to breathe the cool air from the lake, and to take a
survey of the progress of the siege. He was alone, if the
solitary sentinel who paced the mound be excepted, for
the artillerists had hastened also to profit by the temporary suspension of their arduous duties.

Two little spotless flags were abroad, the one on a
salient angle of the fort, and the other on the advanced
battery of the besiegers; emblems of the truce which
existed not only to the acts, but it would seem also to the
enmity of the combatants. Behind these again swung,
heavily opening and closing in silken folds, the rival
standard of England and France.

A hundred gay and thoughtless young Frenchmen
were drawing a net to the pebbly beach; everything

wore the appearance of a day of pleasure rather than an hour stolen from the dangers and toil of a bloody and vindictive warfare.

Duncan had stood in a musing attitude contemplating this scene, when his eyes were directed to the glacis in front of the sally-port already mentioned, by the sound of approachi g footsteps. He walked to an angle of the bastion, and beheld the scout advancing under the custody of a French officer, to the body of the fort. The countenance of Hawk-eye was haggard and care-worn, and his air dejected as though he felt the deepest degradation at having fallen into the power of his enemies. He was without his favourite weapon, and his arms were bound behind him with thongs made of the skin of deer. The young man started with surpise and threw himself down the grassy slope of the bastion; then, moving rapidly across the parade, he was quickly in the presence of the Fort Commander. Munro was pacing his narrow apartment with a disturbed air and gigantic strides as Duncan entered.

'You have anticipated my wishes, Major Heyward,' he said; 'I was about to request this favour.'

'I am sorry to see, sir, that the messenger I so warmly recommended you to send to General Webb has returned in custody of the French. I hope there is no reason to distrust his fidelity.'

'The fidelity of "The Long Rifle" is well known to me,' returned Munro, 'and is above suspicion, though his usual good fortune seems at last to have failed. He did indeed reach Webb but on his return Montcalm has got him, and with the accursed politeness of his nation he has sent him in with a doleful tale "of knowing how I valued the fellow he could not think of retaining him". A Jesuitical way that, Major Duncan Heyward, of telling a man of his misfortunes.'

'But the general and his succour...? They are coming then? The scout has said as much?'

'When? And by what path? For the dunce has omitted to tell me this. No, Major Heyward, there is no intention to advance to our relief. It would seem there is a letter from Webb to this effect which was in the scout's possession when he was intercepted.'

'But sir, what is to be done? I cannot conceal from you that the camp will not much longer be tenable; the walls are crumbling about our ears and provisions begin to fail us. Even the men show signs of discontent.'

'Major Heyward,' said Munro, turning to his youthful associate with the dignity of his years and superior rank, 'I am well aware of the pressing nature of our circumstances, but while there is hope of succour I will defend this fortress. Listen! The Marquis of Montcalm, has, in addition to his other civilities, invited me to a personal interview between the works and his own camp in order, as he says, to impart some additional information. Now I think it would not be wise to show any undue solicitude to meet him and I would employ you, as officer of rank, as my substitute.'

Duncan cheerfully assented to supply the place of the veteran in the approaching interview, and with a roll and beat of the drum, and covered by a little white flag, under the terms of the existing truce, he left the sally-port within ten minutes after his instructions were ended. He was received by the French officer in advance with the usual formalities and immediately accompanied to a distant marquee of the renowned soldier who led the forces of France.

The general of the enemy received the youthful messenger surrounded by his principal officers and by a swarthy band of the native chiefs who had followed him to the field with the warriors of their several tribes. Heyward paused when, in glancing his eyes rapidly over the dark group of the latter, he beheld the malignant countenance of Magua regarding him with the calm but sullen attention of that subtle savage. Recoiling from his evil face, Heyward turned to the hostile commander, who had already advanced a step to receive him.

The Marquis of Montcalm was in the zenith of his fortunes. But, even in that enviable position, he was affable and distinguished as much for his attentions to the forms of courtesy as for that chivalrous courage which, only two years afterwards, induced him to throw away his life on the plains of Abraham. Duncan, in turning his eyes from the malign expression of Magua, suffered them to rest with pleasure on the smiling and polished features, and the noble military air, of the French general.

'Monsieur,' said the latter, 'J'ai beaucoup de plaisir à—bah—où est cet interprète?'

'Je crois, monsieur, qu'il ne sera pas nécessaire,' said Heyward modestly; 'je parle un peu français.'

'Ah! j'en suis bien aise,' said Montcalm, taking Duncan familiarly by the arm and leading him deep into the marquee, a little out of earshot; 'Je déteste ces fripons-là; on ne sait jamais sur quel pié on est avec eux. Eh, bien, monsieur,' he continued still speaking in French; 'though I should have been proud of receiving your commandant, I am very happy that he has seen proper to employ an officer so distinguished, and who, I am sure, is so amiable as yourself.'

Duncan bowed low, pleased with the compliment, in spite of a most heroic determination to suffer no artifice to allure him into the forgetfulness of the interest of his prince; and Montcalm, after a pause of a moment, as if to collect his thoughts, began to discuss terms of surrender.

Duncan's answer was politely firm. 'I fear your excellency has been deceived as to the strength of William Henry, and the resources of its garrison. Furthermore, there is also a powerful force within a few hours march of us which we account upon as part of our means.'

'Some six or eight thousand men,' returned Montcalm with much apparent indifference, 'whom the leader wisely judges to be safer in the works than in the field.'

The battle of wits continued, Duncan trying to make Montcalm reveal the full contents of the intercepted letter; the French leader endeavouring to force surrender. The artifice of neither, however, succeeded; and after a protracted and fruitless interview, Duncan took his leave, favourably impressed with an opinion of the courtesy and talents of the enemy's captain, but as ignorant of what he came to learn as when he arrived. Montcalm followed him as far as the entrance of the marquee, renewing his invitation to the commandant of the fort to give him an immediate meeting in the open ground between the two armies.

There they separated, and Duncan returned to the advance post of the French accompanied as before; whence he instantly proceeded to the fort and to the quarters of his own commander.

Major Heyward found Munro attended by his daughters. Alice sat upon his knee, parting the grey hairs on the forehead of the old man with her delicate fingers; and whenever he affected to frown on her trifling, appeasing his assumed anger by pressing her ruby lips fondly on his wrinkled brow. Cora was seated nigh them, a calm and amused looker-on; regarding the wayward movements of her more youthful sister with that species of maternal fondness which characterised her love for Alice. Of this scene Duncan, who in his eagerness to report his arrival had entered unannounced, stood many moments an unobserved, and delighted spectator. But the quick and dancing eyes of Alice soon caught a glimpse of his figure reflected from a glass, and she sprang blushing from her father's knee, exclaiming aloud:

'Major Heyward!'

'What of the lad?" demanded her father. 'I have sent him to crack a little with the Frenchman. Ha, sir,. you are young and you are nimble. Away with you, ye baggage; as if there were not troubles enough for a soldier without having his camp filled with prattling hussies as yourself!'

Alice laughingly followed her sister, who instantly led the way from an apartment where she perceived their presence was no longer desirable. Munro, instead of demanding the result of the young man's mission, exclaimed:

'They are a pair of excellent girls, Heyward, and such as anyone may boast of.'

'You are not now to learn my opinion of your daughters, Colonel Munro.'

'True, lad, true,' interrupted the impatient old man; 'you were about opening your mind more fully on that matter the day you got in; I am now ready to hear what you have to say.'

'Notwithstanding the pleasure that your assurance gives me, dear sir, I have just now, a message from Montcalm.'

'Let the Frenchman and all his host go to the devil, sir!' exclaimed the hasty veteran. 'He is not yet master of William Henry nor shall he ever be, provided Webb proves himself the man he should. No, sir! Thank heaven we are not yet in such a strait that it can be said Munro is too much pressed to discharge the little domestic duties of his family.'

Heyward, who perceived that his superior took a malicious pleasure in exhibiting his contempt for the message of the French general, was fain to humour a spleen that he knew would be short lived; he therefore replied with as much indifference as could assume on such a subject:

'My request, as you know, sir, went so far as to presume to the honour of being your son.'

'Ay, boy, you found words to make yourself very plainly comprehended. But, let me ask you, sir, have you been as intelligible to the girl?'

'On my honour, no,' exclaimed Duncan warmly; 'there would have been an abuse of a confided trust had I taken advantage of my situation for such a purpose.'

'Your notions are those of a gentleman, Major Heyward, and well enough in their place; but Cora Munro is a maiden too discreet, and of a mind too elevated and improved, to need the guardianship even of a father.'

'Cora!'

'Ay—Cora! We are talking of your pretentions to Miss Munro, are we not, sir?'

'I—I—I was not conscious of having mentioned her name,' said Duncan, stammering.

'And to marry whom, then, did you wish my consent?' demanded the old soldier, erecting himself in the dignity of offended feeling.

'You have another and not less lovely child.'

'Alice!' exclaimed the father in an astonishment equal to that with which Duncan had just repeated the name of her sister.

'Such was the direction of my wishes, sir.'

The young man awaited in silence the result of the extraordinary effect produced by a communication which, as it now appeared, was so unexpected. For several minutes Munro paced the chamber with long and rapid strides, his rigid features working convulsively and every faculty seemingly absorbed in the musings of his own mind. At length he paused directly in front of Heyward, and, riveting his eyes upon those of the other, he said with a lip that quivered violently:

'Duncan Heyward, I have loved you for the sake of him whose blood is in your veins; I have loved you for your own good qualities; and I have loved you because I thought you would contribute to the happiness of my child. Now, you would be my son, Duncan, yet you're ignorant of the history of the man you wish to call your father. Sit ye down, young man, and I will open to you the wounds of a seared heart in as few words as may be suitable.'

By this time the message of Montcalm was much as forgotten by him who bore it as it was by the man for whose ears it was intended.

'You know already, Major Heyward,' began Munro after they had sat down, 'that my family was both ancient and honourable. I was, maybe, such an one as yourself when I plighted my faith to Alice Graham—the only child of a neghbouring laird of some estate. But the connection was disagreeable to her father on more accounts than my poverty. I did, therefore, what an honest man should—restored the maiden her troth, and departed the country in the service of my king. I had seen many regions, and shed much blood in different lands before duty called me to the islands of the West

Indies. There it was my lot to form a connection with one who in time became my wife, and the mother of Cora. She was the daughter of a gentleman of those isles, by a lady whose misfortune it was, if you will,' said the old man proudly, 'to be descended remotely from that unfortunate class who are so basely enslaved to administer to the wants of a luxurious people. Ay, sir, that is a curse entailed on Scotland by her unnatural union with a foreign and trading people. I ask you now openly, sir—can it be that in not wishing Cora as wife, you scorn to mingle the blood of the Heywards with one so degraded—lovely and virtuous though she be?' fiercely demanded the jealous parent.

'Heaven protect me from a prejudice so unworthy of my reason!' returned Duncan. 'The sweetness, the witchery, the beauty of your younger daughter, Colonel Munro, might explain my motives without imputing to me this injustice.'

'Ye are right, sir', returned the old man, again changing his tones to those of gentleness, or rather softness. 'The girl is the image of what her mother was at her years, and before she had become acquainted with grief. When death deprived me of my wife, I returned to Scotland enriched by the marriage; and—would you think it, Duncan!—the suffering angel had remained in the heartless state of celibacy twenty long years, and that for the sake of a man who could forget her! She did more, sir; she overlooked my want of faith, and, all difficulties being now removed, she took me for her husband.'

'And became the mother or Alice?' exclaimed Duncan.

'She did indeed,' said the old man, 'and dearly did she pay for the blessing she bestowed. I had her but a single year, though; a short term of happiness for one who had seen her youth fade in hopeless pining.'

There was something so commanding in the distress of the old man that Heyward did not dare to venture a syllable of consolation. Munro, for his part, sat utterly unconscious of the other's presence for some time. At length he approached his companion with an air of military grandeur and demanded:

'Have you not, Major Heyward, some communication that I should hear from the Marquis de Montcalm?'

Duncan immediately commenced, in an embarrassed voice, the half-forgotten message.

'You have said enough, Major Heyward,' exclaimed the angry old man. 'Enough to make a volume of commentary on French civility. Here has this gentleman invited me to a conference, and when I send him a capable substitute—for ye're all that Duncan, though your years are but few—he answers me with a riddle. I will meet the Frenchman myself then and that without fear or delay as becomes a servant of my royal master. Go, Major Heyward, and give them a flourish of music, and send out a messenger to let them know who is coming.

As soon as the usual ceremonials of a military departure were observed, the veteran and his more youthful companion left the fortress attended by the escort.

They had proceeded only a hundred yards from the works when the little array which attended the French general to the conference was seen issuing from the hollow way which formed the bed of a brook that ran between the batteries of the besiegers and the fort. From the moment that Munro left his own works to appear in front of his enemies, his air had been grand and his step and countenance highly military. The instant he caught a glimpse of the white plume that waved in the hat of Montcalm, his eye lighted and age no longer appeared to possess any influence over his vast and still muscular person.

'Speak to the boys to be watchful, sir,' he said in an undertone to Duncan, 'and to look to their flints and steel, for one is never safe with a servant of one of these Louis. At the same time we will show them the front of men in deep security. Ye'll understand me, Major Heyward!'

He was interrupted by the clamour of a drum from the approaching Frenchmen, which was immediately answered when each party pushed an orderly in front bearing a white flag, and the wary Scotsman halted with his guard close at his back. As soon as this slight salutation had passed, Montcalm moved towards them with a quick but graceful step, baring his head to the veteran and dropping his spotless plume nearly to the earth in courtesy. Neither spoke for a few moments, each regarding the other with curious and interested eyes. Then, as became his superior rank and the nature of the interview, Montcalm broke the silence. After uttering the usual words of greeting, he turned to Duncan and continued with a smile of recognition, speaking always in French:

'I am rejoiced, Monsieur, that you have given us the pleasure of your company on this occasion. There will be no necessity to employ an ordinary interpreter, for in your hands I feel the same security as if I spoke your language myself.'

Duncan acknowledged the compliment; then Montcalm continued: 'I have solicited this interview from your superior, monsieur, because I believe he will allow himself to be persuaded that he has already done everything which is necessary for the honour of his prince and will now listen to the admonitions of humanity. These hills afford us every opportunity of reconnoitring your works, messieurs, and I am possibly as well acquainted with their weak condition as you can be yourselves.'

'Ask the French general if his glasses can reach to the Hudson,' said Munro proudly, 'and if he knows when and where to expect the army of Webb.'

'Let General Webb be his own interpreter,' returned the polite Montcalm, suddenly extending an open letter towards Munro as he spoke.

The veteran seized the offered paper without waiting for Duncan to interpret the speech. As his eye passed hastily over the words, he suffered the paper to fall from his hand for Duncan to glance at its cruel purport. Their common superior, so far from encouraging them to resist, advised a speedy surrender.

'The man has betrayed me!' Munro at length bitterly exclaimed, his head dropping upon his chest like that of a man whose hopes were withered at a single blow.

'Messieurs,' said Montcalm advancing towards them a step in generous interest, 'I have no wish to profit by this letter to humble brave men or to build up a dishonest reputation for myself. Listen to my terms before you leave me. To retain the fort is now impossible for you. It is necessary to the interests of my master that it should be destroyed; but as for yourselves and your brave comrades, there is no privilege dear to a soldier that shall be denied.'

'Our colours?' demanded Heyward.

'Carry them to England and show them to your King.'

'Our arms?'

'Keep them, none can use them better.'

'Our march. The surrender of the place?'

'Shall all be done in a way most honourable to yourselves.'

Duncan now turned to explain those proposals to his commander, who heard them with amazement, and a sensibility that was deeply touched by so unusual and unexpected generosity.

'Go you, Duncan,' he said, 'Go to his marquee and arrange it all. I have lived to see two things in my old age that never did I expect to behold. An Englishman afraid to support a friend and a Frenchman too honest to profit by his advantage.'

So saying, the veteran again dropped his head to his chest and returned slowly towards the fort, while Duncan remained to settle the terms of the capitulation. It was then openly announced that hostilities must cease—Munro having signed a treaty by which the place was to be yielded to the enemy with the morning; the garrison to retain their arms, their colours and their baggage, and consequently, according to military opinion, their honour.

The hostile armies which lay in the wilds of the Horican passed the night of the ninth of August, 1757,

81

in much the same way they would had they encountered on the fairest field of Europe, but during one of those moments of deep silence that prevailed, the canvas that concealed the entrance to a spacious marquee in the French encampment was shoved aside, and a man issued from beneath the drapery into the open air. He was enveloped in a cloak that might have been intended as a protection from the chilling damps of the woods, but which served equally well as a mantle to conceal his person. He was permitted to pass the grenadier who watched over the slumbers of the French commander, without interruption, the man making the usual salute which betokens military deference, as the other passed swiftly through the little city of tents in the direction of William Henry. Whenever this individual encountered one of the numberless sentinels who crossed his path, his answer was prompt, and as it appeared, satisfactory; for he was uniformly allowed to proceed without further interrogation.

With the exception of such repeated but brief interruptions he had moved, silently, from the centre of the camp to its most advanced outposts, when he drew nigh the soldier who held his watch nearest to the works of the enemy. As he approached he received the usual challenge:

'Qui vive?'

'France,' was the reply.

'Le mot d'ordre?'

'La victoire,' said the other, drawing so nigh as to be heard in a loud whisper.

'C'est bien,' returned the sentinel, throwing his musket from the charge to the shoulder. 'Vous vous promenez bien matin, monsieur!'

'Il est nécessaire d'être vigilant, mon enfant', the other observed, dropping a fold in his cloak, and looking the soldier close in the face as he passed him, still continuing his way towards the British fortification. The man started, his arms rattled heavily as he threw them forward in the lowest and most respectful salute; and when he had again recovered his piece, he turned to walk his post, muttering between his teeth:

'Il faut être vigilant, en vérité! Je crois que nous avons la un caporal qui ne dort jamais.'

The officer proceeded, without affecting to hear the words which escaped the sentinel in his surprise; nor did he again pause until he had reached the low strand, and in a somewhat dangerous vicinity to the western water bastion of the fort. Here he took the precaution to place himself against the trunk of a tree, where he leaned for many minutes, and seemed to contemplate the dark and silent mounds of the English works in profound attention. He was in the act of turning on his footsteps when a light sound on the nearest angle of the bastion caught his ear, and induced him to remain.

Just then a figure was seen to approach the edge of the rampart, where it stood, apparently contemplating in its turn the distant tents of the French encampment. Its head was then turned towards the east ast though equally anxious for the appearance of light. The melancholy air, the hour, together with the vast frame of the man who thus leaned musing against the English ramparts, left no doubt in the officer's mind as to the person of the observant spectator. Delicacy, no less than prudence now urged him to retire, and he had moved cautiously round the body of the tree for that purpose when another sound drew his attention, and once more arrested his footsteps. It was a low and almost inaudible movement of the water, and was succeeded by a grating of pebbles one against the other. In a moment he saw a dark form rise, as it were out of the lake, and steal without further noise to the land, within a few feet of the place where he himself stood. A rifle next slowly rose between his eyes and the watery mirror; but before it could be discharged his hand was on the lock.

'Hugh!' exclaimed the savage, whose treacherous aim was so singularly and so unexpectantly interrupted.

Without making any reply, the French officer laid his hand on the shoulder of the Indian, and led him in profound silence to a distance from the spot where their subsequent dialogue might have proved dangerous. Then, throwing open his cloak so as to expose his uniform and the cross of St. Louis which was suspended at his breast, Montcalm sternly demanded:

'What means this? Does not my son know that the hatchet is buried between the English and his Canadian father?'

'What can the Hurons do?' returned the savage, speaking also, though imperfectly in the French language. 'Not a warrior has a scalp and the pale-faces make friends!'

'Ha! Le Renard Subtil! Methinks this is an excess of zeal for a friend who was so late an enemy. How many suns have set since Le Renard struck the war-post of the English?

Montcalm reproved his unreliable ally who eventually stalked sullenly away.

Montcalm lingered long and melancholy on the strand where he had been left by his companion, brooding deeply on the temper which his ungovernable ally had just revealed. He was aware that his fair fame had already been tarnished by one horrid scene, and in circumstances fearfully resembling those under which he now found himself. As he mused he became keenly sensible of the deep responsibility they assume who disregard the means to attain their end, and of all the danger of setting in motion an engine which it exceeds human power to control. Then shaking off a train of reflection which he accounted a weakness in such a moment of triumph, he retraced his steps towards his tent, giving the order as he passed, to make the signal that should rouse the army from its slumbers.

When day dawned, all the usual preparations for a change of masters were ordered, and the French general looked out upon jubilant array. Not so the Anglo-American army, which exhibited all the signs of a hurried and enforced departure. Sullen shoulders shouldered their empty tubes; women and children ran from place to place without purpose; Munro appeared among his silent troops, firm but dejected, and Duncan was touched at the quiet and impressive exhibition of his grief. He had discharged his own duty and he now pressed to the side of the old man to know in what particular he might serve him.

'My daughters,' was the brief but expressive reply.

'Good heavens! Are not arrangements already made for their convenience?'

'Today I am only a soldier, Major Heyward', said the veteran; 'all that you see here claim alike to be my children.'

Duncan had heard enough. Without losing one of those moments which had now become so precious, he flew towards the quarters of Munro in quest of the sisters and found them on the threshold of the low edifice, already prepared to depart. Though the cheeks of Cora were pale and her countenance anxious, she had lost none of her firmness; but the eyes of Alice were red and inflamed and betrayed how long and bitterly she had wept. They both, however, received the young man with undisguised pleasure and willingly accepted his instructions to put themselves into the keeping of David Gamut to whose care they must be entrusted while official duties took their father and Duncan elsewhere.

By this time the signal of departure had been given and the head of the English column was in motion. The sisters started at the sound and glancing their eyes round, they saw the white uniforms of the French grenadiers who had already taken possession of the gates of the fort. At that moment an enormous cloud seemed to pass suddenly above their heads, and looking upward they discovered that they stood beneath the white folds of the standard of France.

'Let us go,' said Cora; 'this is no longer a fit place for the children of an English officer.'

As the confused and timid throng left the protective mounds of the fort, and issued on the open plain, the

85

whole scene was at once presented to their eyes. At a little distance on the right and somewhat in the rear, the French army stood to their arms, Montcalm having collected his parties so soon as his guards had possession of the works. Living masses of the English to the amount in the whole of near three thousand, were moving slowly across the plain towards the common centre, and gradually approached each other as they converged to the point of their march, a vista cut through the lofty trees, where the road to the Hudson entered the forest. Along the sweeping borders of the woods hung a dark cloud of savages, eyeing the passage of their enemies and hovering at a distance, like vultures, who were only kept from swooping on their prey by the presence and restraint of a superior army. A few had straggled among the conquered columns where they stalked in sullen discontent; attentive, though as yet passive, observers of the moving multitude.

But not for long. As the English army with Heyward at its head, was slowly disappearing and the following crowd of women and children moving nearer, the gaudy colours of a shawl attracted the eyes of a wild and untutored Huron. Greedily he snatched at it, hurling to the ground the helpless infant which it folded closely to its mother's bosom. As the woman stood like a statue of despair, the Huron, excited at the sight of the infant's blood, drove his tomahawk into her own brain. At that dangerous moment Magua placed his hands to his mouth and raised the fatal and appalling whoop. The scattered Indians started at the well-known cry, as coursers bound at the signal to quit the goal, and directly there arose such a yell along the plain and through the arches of the wood as seldom burst from human lips before. They who heard it listened with a curdling horror at the heart, little inferior to that dread which may be expected to attend the blasts of the final summons.

More than two thousand raving savages broke from the forest at the signal and threw themselves across the fatal plain with instinctive alacrity. We shall not dwell on the revolting horrors that succeeded. Death was everywhere in his most terrific and revolting aspects. Resistance only served to inflame the murderers who inflicted their furious blows long after their victims were beyond the power of their resentment.

The trained bodies of the troops threw themselves quickly into solid masses, endeavouring to awe their assailants by the imposing appearance of a military front, but with unloaded muskets they had little chance of success.

In such a scene Alice caught a glimpse of the vast form of her father moving rapidly across the plain in the direction of the French army. He was, in truth, proceeding to Montcalm, fearless of every danger, to claim the tardy escort for which he had before conditioned. Fifty glittering axes and barbed spears were offered unheeded at his life, but the savages respected his rank and calmness, even in their fury. Fortunately the vindictive Magua was searching for his victim in the very band the veteran had just quitted.

'Father, father! We are here,' shrieked Alice as he passed at no great distance, without appearing to heed them. 'Come to us, Father, or we die!'

The cry was repeated in terms and tones that might have melted a heart of stone, but it was unanswered. Once, indeed, the old man appeared to catch the sounds, for he paused and listened; but Alice, even as she spoke, had dropped senseless on the earth, and Cora had sunk at her side, hovering in untiring tenderness over her lifeless form. Munro shook his head in disappointment, and proceeded, bent on the high duty of his station.

'Lady,' said Gamut, who helpless and useless as he was had not yet dreamed of deserting his trust. 'It is the jubilee of the devils and this is not a meet place for Christians to tarry in. Let us up and fly.'

'Go,' said Cora, still gazing at her unconscious sister 'save thyself. To me thou canst not be of further use.'

87

David's tall person grew more erect and every feature swelled and seemed to speak with the power of the feelings by which he was governed.

'If the Jewish boy might tame the evil spirit of Saul by the sound of his harp, and the words of sacred song, it may not be amiss,' he said, 'to try the potency of music here.'

Then raising his voice to its highest tones, he poured out a strain so powerful as to be heard even amid the din of that bloody field. More than one savage rushed towards them, thinking to rifle the unprotected sisters of their attire, and bear away their scalps, but when they found this strange and unmoved figure riveted to his post they paused to listen. Astonishment soon changed to admiration, and they passed on to other and less courageous victims, openly expressing their satisfaction with the firmness with which the white warrior sang his death song. Encouraged and deluded by his success David exerted all his powers to extend what he believed so holy an influence. The unwonted sounds caught the ears of a distant savage, who flew, raging from group to group, like one who, scorning to touch the vulgar herd, hunted for some victim more worthy of his renown. It was Magua, who uttered a yell of pleasure when he beheld his ancient prisoners again at his mercy.

'Come,' he said, laying his soiled hands on the dress of Cora, 'the wigwam of the Huron is still open. Is it not better than this place?'

'Away!' cried Cora, veiling her eyes from his revolting aspect.

The Indian laughed tauntingly as he held up his reeking hand, and answered: 'It is red, but it comes from white veins!'

'Monster! There is blood, oceans of blood upon thy soul: thy spirit moved this scene.'

'Magua is a great chief!' returned the exulting savage; 'will the dark-hair go to his tribe?'

'Never! Strike if thou wilt and complete thy revenge.'

He hesitated for a moment, then catching the light and senseless form of Alice in his arms, the subtle Indian moved swiftly across the plains towards the woods.

'Hold!' shrieked Cora, following wildly on his footsteps. 'Release the child! Wretch, what is't you do?'

Magua was deaf to her voice, or rather he knew his power, and was determined to maintain it.

'Stay—lady—stay!' called Gamut after the unconscious Cora. 'The holy charm is beginning to be felt, and soon shall thou see this horrid tumult stilled.'

Perceiving that, in his turn, he was unheeded, the faithful David followed the distracted sister raising his voice again in sacred song, and sweeping the air to the measure with his long arm, in diligent accompaniment. In this manner they traversed the plain through the flying, the wounded and the dead. The fierce Huron was, at any time, sufficient for himself and the victim that he bore; though Cora would have fallen more than once, under the blows of her savage enemies, but for the extraordinary being who stalked in her rear, and who now appeared to the astonished natives gifted with the protecting spirit of madness.

Magua, who knew how to avoid the more pressing danger, and also to elude pursuit, entered the woods through a low ravine, where he quickly found the Narragansets, which the travellers had abandoned so shortly before, awaiting his appearance in custody of a savage as fierce and malign in expression as himself. Making a sign to Cora to mount one of the horses, he placed Alice on the same animal, seized the bridle and commenced his route by plunging deeper into the forst. David, utterly disregarded, mounted another beast and followed.

They soon began to ascend, but as the motion had a tendency to revive the dormant faculties of her sister, the attention of Cora was too much divided between the tenderest solicitude in her behalf, and in listening to the cries which were still too audible on the plain, to note the direction in which they journeyed. When, however, they gained the flattened surface of the mountain top and approached the eastern precipice, she recognized the spot to which she had once before been led under the more friendly auspices of the scout. Here Magua suffered them to dismount, to gaze with horror on the sickening sight below.

The cruel work there was still unchecked. On every side the captured were flying before their relentless persecutors, while the armed columns of the Christian king stood fast in an apathy which has never been explained, and which has left an immovable blot on the otherwise fair escutcheon of their leader. It so far deepened the stain which a previous and very similar event had left upon the reputation of the French commander that it was not entirely erased by his early and glorious death.

7

IN SEARCH OF CORA AND ALICE

The third day from the capture of the fort was drawing to a close, but the business of the narrative must still detain the reader on the shores of the Holy Lake.

It was a scene of wildness and desolation possessed only by stillness and death; and it appeared as if all who had profanely entered it had been stricken, at a blow, by the relentless arm of death. But the prohibition had ceased; and for the first time since the perpetrators of those foul deeds which had assisted to disfigure the scene were gone, living human beings had now presumed to approach the place.

About an hour before the setting of the sun, on the day already mentioned, the forms of five men—three pale-faces and two Indians—might have been seen issuing from the narrow vista of trees, where the path to the Hudson entered the forest, and advancing in the direction of the ruined works.

The reader will perceive at once in these respective characters, the Mohicans and their white friend, the scout, together with Munro and Heyward. It was, in truth, the father in quest of his children, attended by the youth who felt so deep a stake in their happiness, and those brave and trusty foresters who had already proved their skill and fidelity through the trying scenes related.

When Uncas, who moved in front, had reached the centre of the plain, he raised a cry that drew his companions in a body to the spot. The young warrior had halted over a group of females, who lay in a cluster, a confused mass of dead. Notwithstanding the revolting horror of the exhibition Munro and Heyward flew towards the festering heap, endeavouring, with a love that no unseemliness could extinguish, to discover whether any vestiges of those they sought were to be seen among the tattered and many coloured garments.

'I have been on many a shocking field, and have followed a trail of blood for weary miles,' said the scout, 'but never have I seen the hand of the devil so plain as it is here to be seen. What say you, Chingachgouk,' he added in Delaware, 'shall the Hurons boast of this to their women when the deep snows come?'

A gleam of resentment flashed across the dark lineaments of the Mohican chief; he loosened his knife in his sheath, and then, turning calmly from the sight, his countenance settled into a repose as deep as if he never knew the instigation of passion. He was roused by an exclamation from his son.

'Hugh!' exclaimed the young Mohican, rising on the extremities of his feet, and gazing intently in his front.

'What is it, boy?' whispered the scout, lowering his tall form into a crouching attitude, like a panther about to take his leap. 'God send it be a tardy Frencher skulking for plunder. I do believe "Kill-deer" would take an uncommon range, today.'

Uncas, without making any reply, bounded away from the spot, and in the next instant he was seen tearing from a bush, and waving in triumph, a fragment of the green riding veil of Cora. The movement, the exhibition and the cry which again burst from the lips of the young Mohican, instantly drew the whole party about him.

'My child!' said Munro, speaking quick and wildly; 'give me my child!'

'Uncas will try,' was the short and touching answer.

The simple but meaning assurance was lost on the father, who seized the piece of gauze and crushed it in his hand while his eyes roamed fearfully among the bushes, as if he equally dreaded and hoped for the secrets they might reveal.

'Here are no dead,' said Heyward; 'the storm seems to have passed this way.'

'You are right, Uncas,' said the scout, 'The dark-hair has been here and she has fled like a frightened fawn to the wood; none who could fly would remain to be murdered. Let us search for the marks she left; for to Indian eyes I sometimes think, even a humming bird leaves his trail in the air.'

The young Mohican darted away at the suggestion, and the scout had hardly done speaking before the former raised a cry of success from the margin of the forest. On reaching the spot, the anxious party perceived another portion of the veil fluttering on the lower branch of a beech.

'Softly, softly,' said the scout, extending his long rifle in front of the eager Heyward. 'We now know our work but the beauty of the trail must not be deformed. A step too soon may give us hours of trouble. We have them though! That much is beyond denial.'

'Bless ye, bless ye, worthy man!' exclaimed Munro. 'Whither then have they fled, and where are my babes?'

'The path they have taken depends on many chances. If they have gone alone they are quite as likely to move in a circle as straight, and they may be within a dozen miles of us; but if the Hurons, or any of the French Indians, have laid hands on them, it is probable that they are now near the borders of the Canadas.'

'Hugh!' exclaimed Chingachgook, who had been occupied in examining an opening that had evidently been made through the low under-brush which skirted the forest, and who now stood erect as he pointed downwards, in the attitude and with the air of a man who beheld a disgusting serpent.

'Here is the palpable impression of the footstep of a man,' cried Heyward, bending over the indicated spot. 'He has trodden in the margin of this pool and the mark cannot be mistaken. They are captives.'

'Better so than to starve in the wilderness,' returned the scout, 'and they will leave a wider trail. I would wager fifty beaver skins against as many flints that the Mohicans and I enter their wigwams within the month! Stoop to it, Uncas, and try what you can make of the moccasin, for moccasin it plainly is, and no shoe.'

The young Mohican bent over the track, and removing the scattered leaves from around the place, he examined it with much care.

'Le Renard Subtil!' declared Uncas at length.

'Ha! That rampaging devil again! There will never be an end to his loping till "Kill-deer" has said a friendly word to him.'

Heyward reluctantly admitted the truth of this intelligence; then the scout went on:

'Let me get down to it, Uncas; neither book nor moccasin is the worse for having two opinions instead of one.' The scout stooped to the task and instantly added: 'You are right, boy, here is the patch we saw so often in the other chase. Look at it, Sagamore; you measured the prints more than once when we hunted the varmints from Glenn's to the health springs.'

Chingachgook complied, and after finishing his short examination he arose, and with a quiet demeanour he merely pronounced the word:

'Magua.'

'Ay, 'tis settled thing; here then, have passed the dark-hair and Magua.'

'And not Alice?' demanded Heyward.

'Of her we have not yet found the signs,' returned the scout, looking closely round at the trees, the bushes and the ground. 'What have we there, Uncas? Bring hither the thing you see dangling from yonder thorn bush.'

When the Indian had complied, the scout received the prize, and holding it on high, he laughed in his silent but heartfelt manner.

''Tis the tooting weapon of the singer! Now we shall have a trail a priest might travel,' he said. 'Uncas, look for the marks of a shoe that is long enough to uphold six feet two of tottering human flesh. I begin to have hopes of the fellow since he has given up squalling to follow some better trade.'

'At least he has been faithful to his trust,' said Heyward, 'and Cora and Alice are not without a friend.' He turned to Uncas who had been diligently searching the ground. 'Well, boy, any signs of the priest?'

'Here is something like the footstep of one who has worn a shoe; can it be that of our friend?'

'Touch the leaves lightly, or you'll disconcert the formation. That! That is the print of a foot but it is dark-hair'; and small it is, too, for one of such a noble height and grand appearance. There is no woman in the wilderness could leave such a print as that but the dark hair or her sister. We know that the first has been here but where are the signs of the other? Let us push deeper on the trail and if nothing offers, we must go back to the plain and strike another scent. Move on, Uncas, and keep your eyes on the dried leaves. I will watch the bushes while your father shall run with a low nose to the ground. Move on, friends; the sun is getting behind the hills.'

Before they had proceeded many rods, the Indians stopped, and appeared to gaze at some signs on the earth with more than their usual keenness. Both father and son spoke quick and loud, now looking at the object of their mutual admiration, and now regarding each other with the most unequivocal pleasure.

'They have found the little foot!' exclaimed the scout, moving forward without attending further to his own portion of the duty. 'What have we here? An ambushment has been planted in the spot! No, by the truest rifle on the frontiers, here have been them one-sided horses again. Now the whole secret is out and all is plain as the north star at midnight. Yes, here they have mounted. There the beasts have been bound to a sapling in waiting, and yonder runs the broad path away to the north, in full sweep for the Canadas.'

'But still there are no signs of Alice—the younger Miss Munro,' said Duncan.

'Unless the shining bauble Uncas has just lifted from the ground should prove one. Pass it this way, lad, that we may look at it.'

Heyward instantly knew it for a trinket that Alice was fond of wearing, and which he recollected, with the tenacious memory of a lover, to have seen on the fatal morning of the massacre, dangling from the fair neck of his mistress.

'So much the more reason why we should not delay our march,' cried Heyward. 'Let us proceed!'

'Young blood and hot blood, they say, are much the same,' said the scout. 'We are about to outlie for days and nights and to stretch across a wilderness where the feet of men seldom go. We will go back and light our fire tonight in the ruins of the old fort, and in the morning we shall be fresh, and ready to undertake our work like men and not like babbling women or eager boys.'

Heyward saw, by the manner of the scout, that altercation would be useless. Munro had again sunk into that sort of apathy which had beset him since his late overwhelming misfortunes, and from which he was to be apparently roused only by some new and powerful excitement. Making a merit of necessity, the young man took the veteran by the arm and followed in the footsteps of the Indians and the scout, who had already begun to retrace the path which conducted them to the ruins of William Henry, food and rest.

Several hours later the heavens were still studded with stars when Hawk-eye came to arouse the sleepers.

'Come,' he said, making a significant gesture for silence as he turned towards a curtain of the works. 'Let us get into the ditch on this side, and be regardful to step on the stones and fragments of wood as you go.'

With care and patience they succeeded in clambering after the scout until they reached the sandy shore of the Horican.

'That's a trail that nothing but a nose can follow,' said the satisfied scout, looking back along their difficult way. 'Grass is a treacherous carpet for a flying party to tread on, but wood and stone take no print from a moccasin. Shove the canoe in nigher to the land, Uncas; this sand will take a stamp as easily as the butter of the Jarmans on the Mohawk. Softly, lad, softly; it must not touch beach, or the knaves will know by what road we have left the place.'

All sat in silence while the canoe, under the cautious guidance of the Indians, glided over several miles of water. Just as the day dawned they entered the narrows of the lake, and stole swiftly and cautiously among their numberless little islands. It was by this road that Montcalm had retired with his army, and the adventures knew not but he had left some of his Indians in ambush to protect the rear of the forces and to collect the stragglers. They, therefore, approached the passage with the customary silence of their guarded habits.

Chingachgook laid aside his paddle, while Uncas and the scout urged the light vessel through crooked and intricate channels, where every foot that they advanced exposed them to the danger of some sudden rising on their progress. The eyes of the Sagamore moved warily from islet to islet and copse to copse as the canoe proceeded; and when a clearer sheet of water permitted, his keen vision was bent along the bald rocks and impending forests that frowned upon the narrow straight.

The lake now began to expand and their route lay along a wide reach that was lined, as before, by high and ragged mountains.

Instead of following the western shore whither their errand led them, the wary Mohican inclined his course more towards those hills behind which Montcalm was known to have led his army into the formidable fortress of Ticonderoga. There was no apparent reason for this excess of caution. It was, however, maintained for hours until they reached a bay nigh the northern termination of the lake. Here the canoe was driven upon the beach, and the whole party landed. Hawk-eye and Heyward ascended an adjacent bluff, where the former, after considering the expanse of water beneath him, pointed out to the latter a small black object, hovering under a headland, at a distance of several miles.

'Do you see it?' demanded the scout. "Tis a canoe of good birchen bark, and paddled by fierce and crafty Mingoes. These varlets pretend to be chiefly bent on their sundown meal, but the moment it is dark they will be on our trail, as true as hounds on the scent. We must throw them off or our pursuit of Le Renard Subtil may be given up. These lakes are useful at times, especially when the game takes the water. But they give no cover, except it be to the fishes. I little like that smoke which you see worming up along the rock above the canoe. My life on it, other eyes than ours see it, and know its meaning.'

Hawk-eye moved away from the lookout, and descended, musing profoundly to the shore. He communicated the result of his observations to his companions, in Delaware, and a short and earnest consultation succeeded. As a result, the canoe was lifted from the water and borne on the shoulders of the party. They proceeded into the wood, making as broad and obvious a trail as possible. They soon reached a watercourse which they crossed, and continued onward until they came to an extensive and naked rock. At this point, where their footsteps might be expected to be no longer visible, they retraced their route to the brook, walking backwards, with the utmost care. They now followed the bed of the little stream to the lake, into which they immediately launched their canoe again. A low point concealed them from the headland, and the margin of the lake was fringed for some distance with dense and overhanging bushes. Under the cover of these natural advantages they toiled their way with patient industry, until the scout pronounced that he believed that it would be safe once more to land.

The halt continued until evening rendered objects indistinct and uncertain to the eye. Then they resumed their route, and, favoured by the darkness, pushed silently and vigorously towards the western shore. Although the rugged outline of mountain to which they were steering presented no distinctive marks to the eyes of Duncan, the Mohican entered the little haven he had selected with the confidence and accuracy of an experienced pilot.

The boat was again lifted and borne into the woods, where it was carefully concealed under a pile of brush. The adventurers assumed their arms and packs, and the scout announced to Munro and Heyward that he and the Indians were at last in readiness to proceed.

The party had landed on the border of a region that is, even to this day, less known to the inhabitants of the United States than the deserts of Arabia or the steppes of Tartary. It was the sterile and rugged district that separates the tributaries of Champlain from those of the Hudson, the Mohawk and the St. Lawrence. Since the period of our tale, the active spirit of the country has surrounded it with a belt of rich and thriving settlements, though none but the hunter or the savage is ever known, even now, to penetrate its wild recesses.

As Hawk-eye and the Mohicans had, however, often traversed the mountains and the valleys of this vast wilderness, they did not hesitate to plunge into its depths with the freedom of men accustomed to its privations and difficulties. For many hours the travellers toiled on their laborious way, guided by a star or following the direction of some watercourse, until the scout called a halt, and holding a short consultation with the Indians, they lighted their fire and made the usual preparations to pass the remainder of the night where they then were.

After a peaceful night, they proceeded next morning for a few miles, stopping only when Hawk-eye distrusted his own judgement that they had taken the proper scent. Uncas, however, when appealed to by the scout, bounded forward like a deer, and springing up the side of a little acclivity, a few rods in advance, he stood exulting over a spot of fresh earth that looked as if it had recently been upturned by the passage of some heavy animal. The eyes of the whole party followed the unexpected movement, and read their success in the air of triumph that the youth assumed.

"'Tis the trail!' exclaimed the scout, advancing to the spot; 'The lad is keen of sight and quick of wit for his years.'

'See,' said Uncas, pointing north and south at the evident marks of the broad trail on either side of him, 'the dark-hair has gone towards the forest.'

'Hound never ran on a more beautiful scent,' responded the scout, dashing forward at once on the indicated route. 'We are favoured, greatly favoured, and can follow with high noses. Ay, here are both your waddling beasts. This Huron travels like a white general. The fellow is stricken with a judgement and is mad! Look sharp for wheels, Sagamore,' he continued, looking back and laughing in his newly-awakened satisfaction; 'we shall soon have the fool journeying in a coach, and that with three of the best pairs of eyes on the borders in his rear.'

The spirits of the scout and the astonishing success of the chase, in which a circuitous distance of more than forty miles had been passed, did not fail to impart a portion of hope to the whole party. Their advance was rapid, and made with as much confidence, as a traveller would proceed along a wide highway.

By the middle of the afternoon, they had passed the Scaroon, and were following the route of the declining sun. After descending an eminence to a low bottom, through which a swift stream glided, they suddenly came to a place where the party of Le Renard had made obviously a halt. But while the earth was trodden, and the footsteps of both men and beasts were so plainly visible around the place, the trail appeared to have suddenly ended.

It was easy to follow the tracks of the Narragansets, but they seemed only to have wandered without guides, or any other object than the pursuit of food. At length Uncas, who with his father had endeavoured to trace the route of the horses, came upon a sign of their presence that was quite recent. Before following the clue, he communicated his success to his companions; and while the latter were consulting on the circumstances, the youth reappeared leading the two fillies, with their saddles broken and the housings soiled as though they had been permitted to run at will for several days.

'What should this prove?' said Duncan, turning pale and glancing his eyes around him, as if he feared the brush and leaves were about to give up some horrid secret.

'That our march has come to a quick end, and that we are in an enemy's country,' returned the scout. 'It is true that the horses are here, but the Hurons are gone; let us then hunt for the path by which they departed'.

Hawk-eye and the Mohican now applied themselves to their task in good earnest. A circle of a few hundred feet in circumference was drawn, and each of the party took a segment for his portion. The examination, however, resulted in no discovery. The impressions of footsteps were numerous, but they all appeared like those of men who had wandered about the spot without any design to quit it.

At length Uncas, whose activity had enabled him to achieve his portion of the task the soonest, raked the earth across the turbid little rill which ran from the spring, and diverted its course into another channel. So soon as its narrow bed below the dam was dry, he stooped over it with keen and curious eyes. A cry of exultation immediately announced the success of the young warrior. The whole party crowded to the spot, where Uncas pointed out the impression of a moccasin in the moist alluvium.

'The lad will be an honour to his people.' said Hawkeye, regarding the trail with as much admiration as a naturalist would expend on the tusk of a mammoth or the rib of a mastodon: 'aye, and a thorn in the sides of the Hurons. Yet that is not the footstep of an Indian! The weight is too much on the heel and the toes are squared as though one of the French dancers had been in, pigeon-winging his tribe! Run back, Uncas, and bring me the size of the singer's foot. You will find a beautiful print of it just opposite yon rock ag'in the hillside.'

While the youth was engaged in this commission, the scout and Chingachgook were attentively considering the impressions. The measurements agreed, and the former unhesitatingly pronounced that the footstep was that of David, who had, once more, been made to exchange his shoes for moccasins.

'I can now read the whole of it as plainly as if I had seen the arts of Le Subtil,' he added; 'the singer being a man whose gifts lay chiefly in his feet and his throat, was made to go first, and the others have trod in his steps, imitating their formation.'

'But,' cried Duncan, 'I see no signs of...'

'The gentle ones,' interrupted the scout; 'the varlet has found a way to carry them until he supposed he had thrown any followers off the scent. My life on it, we shall see their pretty little feet again before many rods go by.'

The whole party now proceeded, following the course of the rill, keeping anxious eyes on the regular impressions, More than half a mile was passed before the rill rippled close around the base of an extensive and dry rock. Here they paused to make sure that the Hurons had not quitted the water.

It was fortunate they did so. For the quick and active Uncas had found the impression of a foot on a bunch of moss, where it would seem an Indian had inadvertently trodden. Pursuing the direction given by this discovery, he entered the neighbouring thicket and struck the trail, as fresh and obvious as it had been before they had reached the spring. Another shout announced the good fortune of the youth to his companions, and at once terminated the search.

'Will this assist in explaining the difficulty?' said Heyward, pointing towards the fragments of a sort of hand-barrow that had been rudely constructed of boughs, and bound together with withes, and which now seemed carelessly cast aside as useless.

"Tis explained!' cried the delighted Hawk-eye. 'If them varlets have passed a minute, they have spent hours in trying to fabricate a lying end to their trail! Here we have three pairs of moccasins and two of little feet. Pass me the thong of buck skin, Uncas, and let me take the length of this foot. By the Lord! It is no longer than a child's, and yet both the maidens are tall and comely. That Providence is partial in its gifts, for its own wise reasons, the best and most contented of us must allow.'

'The tender limbs of my daughters are unequal to these hardships,' said Munro, looking at the light footsteps of his children with a parent's love. 'We shall find their fainting forms in this desert.'

'Of that there is little cause of fear,' returned the scout, slowly shaking his head, 'This is a firm and straight, though a light step, and not over long.'

From such undeniable testimony did the practised woodsman arrive at the truth, with nearly as much certainty and precision as if he had been a witness of all those events which his ingenuity so easily elucidated. Cheered by these assurances, and satisfied by a reasoning that was so obvious, while it was so simple, the party resumed its course, after making a short halt to take a hurried meal.

When the meal was ended, the scout cast a glance upwards at the setting sun, and pushed forward with a rapidity which compelled Heyward and the still vigorous Munro to exert all their muscles to equal. The route now lay along the bottom which has already been mentioned. As the Hurons had made no further efforts to conceal their footsteps, the progress of the pursuers was no longer delayed by uncertainty. Before an hour had elapsed, however, the speed of Hawk-eye had sensibly abated and he waited for the whole party to come up.

'I scent the Hurons,' he said, speaking to the Mohicans. 'Yonder is open sky through the tree-tops and we are getting too nigh their encampment. Sagamore, you will take the hillside to the right; Uncas will bend along the brook to the left, while I will try the trail. If anything should happen, the call will be three croaks of a crow. I saw one of the birds fanning himself in the air, just beyond the dead oak—another sign that we are touching the encampment.'

The Indians departed their several ways without reply, while Hawk-eye cautiously proceeded with the two officers. Heyward soon pressed to the side of their guide, eager to catch an early glimpse of those enemies he had pursued with so much toil and anxiety. His companion told him to steal to the edge of the wood, which, as usual, was fringed with a thicket, and wait his coming, for he wished to examine certain suspicious signs a little to one side. Duncan obeyed and soon found himself in a situation to command a view which he found as extraordinary as it was novel.

The trees of many acres had been felled, and the glow of a mild summer's evening had fallen on the clearing, in beautiful contrast to the grey of the forest. A short distance from the place where Duncan stood, the stream had seemingly expanded into a little lake, covering most of the low land from mountain to mountain. The water fell out of this wide basin in a cataract so regular and gentle that it appeared rather to be the work of human hands than fashioned by nature. A hundred earthern dwellings stood on the margin of the lake, and even in its water, as though the latter had overflowed its usual banks. Their rounded roofs, admirably moulded for defence against the weather, denoted more industry and foresight than the natives were wont to bestow on their regular habitations much less on those they occupied for the temporary purposes of hunting and war. In short, the whole village or town, whichever it may be termed, possessed more of method and neatness of execution than white men had been accustomed to believe belonged ordinarily to the Indian habits. It appeared, however, to be deserted. At least, so thought Duncan for many minutes, but at length he fancied he discovered several human forms advancing towards him on all-fours, and apparently dragging in their train some heavy formidable engine. Just then a few dark-looking heads leaned out of the dwellings, and the place seemed suddenly alive with beings, which, however, glided from cover to cover so swiftly as to allow no opportunity of examining their humours or pursuits. Alarmed at these suspicious and inexplicable movements, he was about to attempt the signal of the crows when the rustling of leaves at hand drew his eyes in another direction.

The young man recoiled a few paces instinctively when he found himself within a hundred yards of a stranger Indian. Recovering himself on the instant, he remained stationary, an attentive observer of the other's motions.

An instant of calm observation served to assure Duncan that he was undiscovered. The native, like himself, seemed occupied in considering the low dwellings of the village and the stolen movements of its inhabitants. It was impossible to discover the expression of his features through the grotesque mask of paint under which they were concealed, though Duncan fancied it was rather melancholy than savage. His head was shaved as usual, with the exception of the crown, from whose tuft three or four faded feathers from a hawk's wing were loosely dangling.

Duncan was still curiously observing the person of his neighbour when the scout stole silently to his side and stretched forward his long neck as if to assist a scrutiny that was already intensively keen.

'The imp is not a Huron nor of the army of Canada tribes,' he said. 'And yet you see by his clothes that the knave has been plundering a white. Here, do you keep him under your rifle while I creep in behind through the bush and take him alive. He may have some information to impart.'

In the next moment he was concealed by the leaves, then reappeared, creeping along the earth from which his dress was hardly distinguishable, directly in the rear of his intended captive, who was wholly absorbed in watching the movements about the gloomy lake. Having reached within a few yards of the latter, Hawk-eye arose to his feet silently, his uplifted hand ready to strike. Then without any apparent reason to the watching Duncan, the hand was withdrawn from its menacing position and its owner indulged in a long, though silent, fit of merriment. Thereafter, instead of grasping his victim by the throat, he merely tapped the stranger lightly on the shoulder in the most amiable of ways and exclaimed aloud:

'How now, friend! Have you a mind to teach the beavers how to sing?'

8

ALICE RESCUED

The reader may better imagine than we describe the
surprise of Heyward. His lurking Indians were suddenly
converted into four-footed beasts; his lake into a
beaver pond; his cataract into a dam, constructed by
those industrious and ingenious quadrupeds; and a
suspected enemy into his friend, David Gamut, the
master of psalmody. The presence of the latter created
so many unexpected hopes relative to the sisters that,
without a moment's hesitation, the young man broke
out of his ambush and sprang forward to join the two
principal actors in the scene.

The merriment of Hawk-eye was not easily appeased.
Without ceremony, and with a rough hand, he twirled
the supple Gamut around on his heel, and more than
once affirmed that the Hurons had done themselves
great credit in the fashion of his costume.

'We see that you are safe. Now tell us what has
become of the maidens,' he asked.

'They are captives to the heathen,' said David, 'and,
though greatly troubled in spirit, enjoying comfort
and safety in the body.'

'Both?' demanded the breathless Heyward.

'Even so. Though our wayfaring has been sore, and
our sustenance scanty, we have had little other cause
for complaint, except the violence done our feelings
by being thus led in captivity into a far land.'

'Where is the knave, Magua?' bluntly interrupted
the scout.

'He hunts the moose today with his young men, and tomorrow, as I hear, they pass farther into these forests and nigher to the borders of Canada. The elder maiden is conveyed to a neighbouring people, whose lodges are situated beyond yonder black pinnacle of rock; while the younger is detained among the women of the Hurons, whose dwellings are but two short miles hence on a table-land, where the fire has done the office of the axe and prepared the place for their recepetion.

'And why are you permitted to go at large, unwatched?

'Because of the power of psalmody, which, though it was suspected in the terrible business of that field of blood, has recovered its influence over the souls of the heathen. Hence I am suffered to come and go at will.'

The scout laughed at David's last remark and handed him back his pitch pipe which he received with a strong expression of pleasure. He then narrated his adventures.

Magua had waited on the mountain until a safe moment to retire presented itself, when he had descended and taken the route along the western side of the Horican in the direction of the Canadas. At night, the utmost care had been taken of the captives, both to prevent injury from the damps of the woods, and to guard against an escape» At the spring the horses were turned loose as had been seen ; and notwithstanding the remoteness and length of their trail, the artifices already named were resorted to. At the arrival at the encampment of his people, Magua, in a policy seldom departed from, separated his prisoners. Cora had been sent to a tribe that temporarily occupied an adjacent valley, though David was far too ignorant of the customs and history of the natives to be able to declare anything satisfactory concerning their name or character. He only knew they had not engaged in the late expedition against William Henry; that like the Hurons themselves, they were allies of Montcalm;

and that they maintained an amicable, though a watchful, intercourse with the warlike and savage people whom chance had, for a time, brought in such close and disagreeable contact with themselves.

The Mohicans and the scout listened to his interrupted and imperfect narrative with an interest that obviously increased as he proceeded; and it was while attempting to explain the pursuits of the community in which Cora was detained that the latter abruptly demanded:

'Did you see the fashion of their knives? Were they of English or French formation?'

'My thoughts were bent on no such vanities, but rather mingled in consolation with those of the maidens.'

'The time may come when you will not consider the knife of a savage such a despisable vanity', returned the scout with a strong expression of contempt for the other's dullness. 'Had they held their corn-feast? Or can you say anything of the totems of the tribe?'

'Of corn we had many and plentiful feasts; for the grain, being in the milk, is both sweet to the mouth and comfortable to the stomach. Of the totem I know not the meaning, but I have seen strange and fantastic images drawn in their paint, of which their admiration and care savoured of spiritual pride; especially one, and that too, a foul and loathsome object.'

'Was it a serpent?' quickly demanded the scout.

'Much the same. It was in the likeness of an' abject and creeping tortoise.

'Hugh!' exclaimed both the attentive Mohicans in one breath, while the scout shook his head with the air of one who has made an important, but by no means pleasant, discovery. Then the father spoke in the language of the Delawares, his gestures impressive and at times energetic. Once he lifted his arm on high and, as it descended, the action threw aside the folds of his light mantle, revealing to Duncan that the animal just mentioned was beautifully, though faintly, worked in a blue tint on the swarthy breast of the chief. All that he had ever heard of the violent separation of the vast tribes of the Delawares rushed across his mind, and his thoughts were now confirmed by the scout, who spoke:

'We have found that which may be good or evil to us, as Heaven disposes. The Sagamore Chingachgook is of the high blood of the Delawares and is the great chief of their Tortoises. That some of his stock are among the people of whom the singer tells us is plain by his words. 'Tis a long and melancholy tradition, and one I like little to think of, for it is not to be denied that the evil has been mainly done amongst them by men with white skins. But it has ended with turning the tomahawk of brother against brother, and brought the Mingo and the Delaware to travel in the same path.'

'You thus suspect that it is a portion of that people among whom Cora resides?'

The scout nodded his head in assent, though he seemed anxious to waive further discussion of a subject that appeared painful. The impatient David now made several hasty and desperate propositions to attempt the release of the sisters; but the scout, after suffering the ardour of the lover to expend itself a little, found means to convince him of the folly of precipitation.

'It would be well,' he added, 'to let David go in again as usual, and for him to tarry in the lodges, giving notice to the gentle ones of our approach, until we call him out by signal. Then when—'

'Stop!' interrupted Heyward. 'I will accompany him. I too can play the madness, the fool, the hero, in short any or everything to rescue her I love. You have the means of disguise; change me, paint me, too, if you will; in short, alter me to anything—a fool!'

Hawk-eye regarded the young man in speechless amazement, but Duncan, hitherto submissive, now asserted the superior with a manner that was not easily resisted.

'Listen! You have heard from this faithful follower of the captives that the Indians are of two tribes, if not of different nations. With one whom you think to be a branch of the Delawares is she whom you call "Dark hair", the other and younger of the ladies is undeniably with our declared enemies, the Hurons. It becomes my youth and rank to attempt the latter adventure. While you, therefore, are negotiating with your friends for the release of the one sister, I will effect that of the other, or die.'

As he listened, Hawk-eye's humour suddenly altered and he lent himself to the scheme.

'Come,' he said with a good-humoured smile. 'Chingachgook has as many different paints as the engineer officer's wife and can use them too. On my life he can soon make a natural fool of you and that well to your liking.'

The Mohican readily undertook the office and drew with great dexterity the fantastic shadow that the natives were accustomed to consider as the evidence of a friendly jocular disposition. Every line that could possibly be interpreted into a secret inclination for war was carefully avoided, and as Duncan was already sufficiently disguised in his dress, there certainly did exist some reason for believing that, with his knowledge of French, he might pass for a juggler from Ticonderoga, straggling among the allied and friendly tribes.

When he was thought to be sufficiently painted, the scout gave him much friendly advice, concerted signals and appointed the place where they should meet in the event of mutual success. He acquainted him too, in private, with his intention to leave the veteran Munro in some safe encampment in charge of Chingachgook, while he and Uncas pursued their inquiries among the people they had reason to believe were Delawares. Then renewing his cautions and advice, he concluded by saying with a solemnity and warmth of feeling with which Duncan was deeply touched:

'And now God bless you! You have shown a spirit that I like; for it is the gift of youth, more especially one of warm blood and a stout heart.'

Duncan shook his worthy and reluctant associate warmly by the hand, once more recommended his ancient friend to his care, and returning his good wishes, he motioned to David to proceed. Hawk-eye gazed after the spirited and adventurous young man for several moments in open admiration; then shaking his head doubtingly, he turned and led his own division of the party into the concealment of the forest.

The route taken by Duncan and David lay directly across the clearing of the beavers and along the margin of their pond. After making nearly a semicircle around the water, they diverged from the watercourse and began to ascend to the level of a slight elevation of that bottom land over which they journeyed, and together they pursued their way towards what David was sometimes wont to call 'the tents of the Philistines.'

It is unusual to find an encampment of the natives, like those of the more instructed whites, guarded by the presence of armed men. Well informed of the approach of every danger while it is yet at a distance, the Indian generally rests secure under his knowledge of the signs of the forest, and the long and difficult paths that separate him from those he has most reason to dread. But the enemy who, by any lucky concurrence of accidents, has found means to elude the vigilance of the scouts, will seldom meet with sentinels nearer to home to sound the alarm. In addition to this general usage, the tribes friendly to the French knew too well the weight of the blow that had just been struck, to apprehend any immediate danger from the hostile nations that were tributary to the crown of Britain.

When Duncan and David, therefore, found themselves in the centre of some children who played, it was without the least previous intimation of their approach. But so soon as they were observed the whole juvenile pack raised, by common consent, a shrill and warning whoop, and then sank, as it were by magic, from before the sight of their visitors. The cry of the children had drawn a dozen warriors to the door of the nearest lodge, where they stood clustered in a dark savage group gravely awaiting the nearer approach of those who had unexpectedly come upon them.

David, in some measure familiarized to the scene, led the way with a steadiness that no slight obstacle was likely to disconcert into this very building. It was the principle edifice of the village, though roughly constructed of the bark and branches of trees, being the lodge where the tribe held its councils and public meetings during their temporary residence on the borders of the English province. Duncan's blood curdled as, following his companion's footsteps closely, he pursued his way into the centre of the lodge, but his exterior did not betray the weakness.

So soon as their visitor had passed, the observant warriors fell back from the entrance, and arranging themselves about him they seemed patiently to await the moment when it might comport with the dignity of the stranger to speak. A flaring torch was burning in the place, and sent its red glare from face to face as it waved in the currents of air. Duncan profited by its light to read the probable character of his reception in the countenances of his hosts.

At length, one whose hair was beginning to be sprinkled with grey, but whose sinewy limbs and firm tread announced that he was still equal to the duties of manhood, advanced out of the gloom of a corner, whither he had probably posted himself to make his observations unseen, and spoke. He used the language of the Wyandots or Hurons; his words were, consequently, unintelligible to Heyward, though they seemed, by the gestures that accompanied them, to be uttered more in courtesy than in anger. The latter shook his head, and made a gesture indicative of his inability to reply.

'Do none of my brothers speak the French or the English?' he said in the former language, looking about him from countenance to countenance in hopes of finding a nod of assent.

Though more than one had turned as if to catch the meaning of his words, they remained unanswered.

'I should be grieved to think,' continued Duncan, speaking slowly and using the simplest French of which he was the master, 'to believe that none of this wise and brave nation understand the language that the "Grand Monarque" uses when he talks to his children. His heart would be heavy did he believe his red warriors paid him so little respect.'

At length the same warrior who had addressed him replied by dryly demanding, in the language of the Canadas, what purpose had brought him thither.

'I who am a man that knows the art of healing, am come at the bidding of our Canada father to his children, the red Hurons of the great lakes, and ask if any are sick.'

This idea of the newcomer as a witch-doctor appeared to satisfy the onlookers and Duncan began to breathe more freely believing that the weight of his examination was past; and as he had already prepared a simple and probable tale to support his pretended occupation, his hopes of ultimate success grew brighter.

After a silence of a few moments, as if adjusting his thoughts in order to make a suitable answer to the declaration their guest had just given, another warrior arose and placed himself in an attitude to speak. While his lips were yet in the act of parting, a low but fearful sound arose from the forest, and was immediately succeeded by a high shrill yell, that was drawn out until it equalled the longest and most plaintive howl of a wolf. The sudden and terrible interruption caused Duncan to start from his seat, unconscious of everything but the effect produced by so frightful a cry. At the same moment the warriors glided in a body from the lodge, and the outer air was filled with loud shouts that nearly drowned those awful sounds that were

114

still ringing beneath the arches of the woods. Unable to command himself, Duncan broke from the lodge and presently stood without, gazing at a line of warriors issuing from the woods and advancing slowly towards the dwellings.

The startling sound that Duncan had heard were what the whites have, not inappropriately, called the 'death-hallo,' and each repetition of the cry was intended to announce to the tribe the fate of an enemy. Thus far the knowledge of Heyward assisted him in the explanation; and as he now knew that the interruption was caused by the unlooked-for return of a successful war party, bearing a pole from which were suspended several human scalps and preceded by two prisoners, every disagreeable sensation was quieted in inward congratulations for the opportune relief and in significance it conferred on himself.

When at a distance of a few hundred feet from the lodges, the newly-arrived warriors and their prisoners halted. Their plaintive and terrific cry, which was intended to represent equally the wailings of the dead and the triumph of the victors, had entirely ceased. One of their number now called aloud, in words that were far from appalling though not more intelligible to those for whose ears they were intended than their expressive yells. It would be difficult to convey a suitable idea of the savage ecstasy with which the news thus imparted was received. The whole encampment, in a moment, became a scene of the most violent bustle and commotion. The warriors drew their knives and, flourishing them, they arranged themselves in two lines, forming a lane that extended from the war party to the lodges. Even the squaws and children seized clubs and tomahawks and rushed eagerly to act their part in the game that was about to be played when the prisoners were forced to race between the two lines of torturing weapons.

Piles of brush already lit by an eldery squaw gave an eerie light that was not strong enough to render their features distinct, though it was quite evident that they were governed by different emotions. While one stood erect and firm, the other bowed his head as if palsied by terror or stricken with shame. The high-spirited Duncan felt a powerful impulse of admiration towards the former. He watched his slightest movement with eager eyes and was persuaded that if the powers of man could bear one harmless through so severe a trial, the youthful captive before him might hope for success in the hazardous race he was to run.

Just then the signal yell was given and the momentary quiet was broken by a burst of cries on all sides. The most abject of the two victims continued motionless, but the other bounded from the place at the cry with the swiftness of a deer. Instead of rushing through the dangerous defile, and before time was given for a single blow, he turned short and, leaping the heads of a row of children, gained at once the exterior and safer side of the formidable array. The whole of the excited multitude broke from their order and spread themselves about the place in wild confusion.

No breathing space was allowed the fugitive. Driven back from the forest into the centre of his relentless persecutors, he turned like a headed deer, shot with the swiftness of an arrow through the pillar of forked flame and appeared on the opposite side of the clearing, where now and then Duncan caught a glimpse of a light form clearing the air in some desperate bound. Suddenly the multitude rolled backwards and approached the spot where he himself stood, and the fugitive as if aware no danger was to be apprehended from the young soldier, nearly brushed his person in flight. A tall and powerful Huron pressed close on the fugitives heels, with an uplifted arm menaced a fatal blow. Duncan thrust forth a foot, and the shock precipitated the eager savage headlong, many feet in advance of his intended victim. The latter, quick as thought, turned and clung to a small painted post which stood before the door of the principal lodge.

Apprehensive that the part he had taken in the escape might prove fatal to himself, Duncan left the place.

without delay. He followed the crowd which drew nigh the lodges, gloomy and sullen like any other multitude that had been disappointed in an execution. Curiosity, or perhaps a better feeling, induced him to approach the stranger. He found him standing with one arm cast about the protecting post, and breathing thick and hard after his exertions, but disdaining to allow a single sign of suffering to escape. His person was now protected by immemorial and sacred usage until the tribe in council had deliberated and determined on his fate. It was not difficult, however, to foretell the result, if any presage could be drawn from the feelings of those who crowded the place.

There was no term of abuse known to the Huron vocabulary that the disappointed women did not lavishly expend on the successful stranger. They flouted at his efforts and told him with bitter scoffs that his feet were better than his hands, and that he merited wings while he knew not the use of an arrow or a knife. To all this the captive made no reply, but was content to preserve an attitude in which dignity was singularly blended with disdain. Exasperated as much by his composure as by his good fortune, their words became unintelligible, and were succeeded by shrill piercing yells. Just then the crafty squaw, who had taken the necessary precaution to fire the piles, made her way through the throng.

'Look you, Delaware,' she said, snapping her fingers in his face, 'your nation is a race of women and a hoe is better fitted to your hands than the gun! Your squaws are the mothers of deer; but if a bear or a wild-cat, or a serpent was born among you, ye would flee. The Huron girls shall make you petticoats and we will find you a husband.'

Infuriated at the self-command of the captive, the woman placed her arms akimbo, and throwing herself into a posture of defiance, she broke out anew in a torrent of words that no art of ours could commit successfully to paper, yet without causing a muscle to vibrate in the motionless figure of the stranger. The effect of his indifference began to extend its effect to the other spectators, and a youngster, who was just quitting the condition of a boy to enter the state of manhood, attempted to assist the termagant by flourishing his tomahawk before their victim, and adding his empty boasts to the taunts of the woman. Then indeed, the captive turned his face momentarily towards the light and looked down on the stripling with an expression that was superior to contempt. But the change of posture had permitted Duncan to exchange glances with the form and piercing eyes of Uncas.

Breathless with amazement, and heavily oppressed with the critical situation of his friend, Heyward recoiled before the look, trembling lest its meaning might in some unknown manner hasten the prisoner's fate. There was not, however, any instant cause for such apprehension. Just then a warrior forced his way into the exasperated crowd. Motioning the women and children aside with a stern gesture, he took Uncas by the arm and led him towards the door of the council lodge. Thither all the chiefs and most of the distinguished warriors followed, among whom the anxious Heyward found means to enter without attracting any dangerous attention to himself.

A few minutes were consumed by disposing of those present in a manner suitable to their rank and influence in the tribe. An order very similar to that adopted in the preceding interview was observed, the aged and superior chiefs occupying the area of the spacious apartment, within the powerful light of a glaring torch, while their juniors and inferiors were arranged in the background, presenting a dark line of swarthy and marked visages. In the very centre of the lodge, immediately under an opening that admitted the twinkling light of one or two stars, stood Uncas, calm, elevated and collected.

The case was different with the individual whom Duncan had observed to stand forth with his friend previously to the desperate trial of speed and who, instead of joining in the chase, had remained throughout its turbulent uproar like a cringing statue expressive of shame and disgrace. Heyward profited by the first opportunity to gaze in his face, secretly apprehensive he might find the features of another acquaintance; but they proved to be those of a stranger, and, what was still more inexplicable, of one who bore all the distinctive marks of a Huron warrior.

When each individual had taken his proper station, and silence reigned in the place, the grey-haired chief already introduced to the reader spoke aloud in the language of the Lenni Lenape.

'Delaware,' he said, 'though one of a nation of women, you have proved yourself a man. I would give you food, but he who eats with a Huron should become his friend. Rest in peace till the morning sun, when our last words shall be spoken.'

'Seven nights and as many summer days have I fasted on the trail of the Hurons,' Uncas coldly replied. 'The children of the Lenape know how to travel the path of the just without hungering to eat.'

'Two of my young men are in pursuit of your companion,' resumed the other, without appearing to regard the boast of his captive. 'When they get back, then will our wise men say to you "live" or "die".'

'Has a Huron no ears?' scornfully replied Uncas. 'Twice since he has been your prisoner has the Delaware heard a gun that he knows. Your young men will never come back.'

Duncan who understood the Mohican to allude to the fatal rifle of the scout, bent forward in earnest observation of the effect it might produce on the conquerors but the chief was content with simply retorting: 'If the Lenape are so skilful, why is one of their bravest warriors here?'

'He followed in the steps of a flying coward, and fell into a snare. The cunning beaver may be caught.'

As Uncas thus replied, he pointed towards the solitary Huron but without deigning to bestow any other notice on so worthy an object. The words of the answer and the air of the speaker produced a strong sensation among his auditors. Every eye rolled sullenly towards the individual indicated by the simple gesture, and a low, threatening murmur passed through the crowd. In the meantime the more aged in the centre communed with each other in short and broken sentences. Not a word was uttered that did not convey the meaning of the speaker in the simplest and most energetic form. Again a long and deeply solemn pause took place. It was known by all present to be the grave precursor of a weighty and important judgement. The silence was finally broken by the aged warrior so often named. He rose from the earth and passing by the immovable from of Uncas, placed himself in a dignified attitude before the offender.

At that moment the withered squaw moved into the circle in a slow sidling sort of dance, holding the torch and muttering the indistinct words of what might have been a species of incantation.

Approaching Uncas, she held the blazing brand in such a manner as to cast its red glare on his person, and to expose the slightest emotion of his countenance. The Mohican maintained his firm and haughty attitude, and his eye, so far from deigning to meet her inquisitive look, dwelt steadily on the distance. Satisfied with her examination she left him with a slight expression of pleasure, and proceeded to practise the same trying experiment on her delinquent countryman.

The young Huron was in his war-paint and very little of a finely moulded form was concealed by his attire. The light rendered every line and joint discernible, and Duncan turned away in horror when he saw they were writhing in irrepressible agony. The woman was commencing a low and plaintive howl at the sad and shameful spectacle, when the chief put forth his hand and gently pushed her aside.

'Reed-that-bends,' he said, addressing the young culprit by name in his proper language, 'though the Great Spirit had made you pleasant to the eyes, it would have been better that you had not been born. Your tongue is loud in the village, but in battle it is still. None of my young men strike the tomahawk deeper into the war-post—none of them so lightly on the Yengeese. The enemy know the shape of your back, but they have never seen the colour of your eyes. Three times have they called on you to come, and as often did you forget to answer. Your name will never be mentioned again in the tribe—it is already forgotten.'

As the chief slowly uttered thise words, pausing impressively between each sentence, the culprit raised his face in deference to the other's rank and years. Shame, horror and pride struggled in its lineaments. His eye, which was contracted with inward anguish, gleamed on the persons of those whose breath was his fame; and the latter emotion for an instant predominated. He rose to his feet, and baring his bosom, looked steadily on the keen, glittering knife that was already upheld by his inexorable judge. As the weapon passed slowly into his heart he even smiled, as if in joy at having found death less dreadful than he had anticipated, and fell heavily on his face at the feet of the rigid and unyielding form of Uncas.

The aged squaw gave a loud and plaintive yell, and dashed the torch she had been holding to the earth and buried everything in darkness. The whole shuddering group of spectators glided from the lodge like troubled sprites and Duncan thought that he and the yet throbbing body of the victim of an Indian judgement had now become its only tenants.

A single moment served to convince the youth that he was mistaken. A hand was laid with a powerful pressure on his arm, and the low voice of Uncas muttered in his ears:

'The Hurons are dogs. The sight of a coward's blood can never make a warrior tremble. The "Grey-Head" and the Sagamore are safe, and the rifle of Hawk-eye is not asleep. Go—Uncas and the "Open Hand" are now strangers. It is enough.'

Heyward would have gladly heard more, but a gentle push from his friend urged him towards the door and admonished him of the danger that might attend the discovery of their whispered conversation. Slowly he quitted the place and mingled with the throng that hovered nigh. Occasionally a brighter gleam than common glanced into the lodge and exhibited the figure of Uncas still maintaining its upright attitude near the figure of the dead Huron.

A knot of warriors soon entered the place again, and, reissuing, they bore the senseless remains into the adjacent woods. After this, Duncan, wandered among the lodges unquestioned and unnoticed, endeavouring to find some trace of her on whose behalf he incurred the risk he ran. Abandoning a species of inquiry that proved fruitless, he returned to the lodge where a hasty glance sufficed to tell him that, though Uncas still remained where he had left him, David had not reappeared. No other restraint was imposed on the former than the watchful looks of a young Huron who had placed himself at hand, though an armed warrior leaned against the post that formed one side of the narrow doorway. In every other respect the captive seemed at liberty.

Duncan had not long occupied a seat, wisely taken a little in the shade, when another of the elder warriors, who spoke the French language, addressed him:

'My Canada father does not forget his children,' said the Chief. 'I thank him. An evil spirit lives in the wife of one of my young men. Can the cunning stranger frighten him away?'

Heyward answered with suitable mystery:

'Spirits differ. Some yield to the power of wisdom, while others are too strong.'

'My brother is a great medicine,' said the cunning savage 'He will try?'

A gesture of assent was the answer. The Huron was content with the assurance, and, resuming, his pipe, awaited the proper moment to move. The impatient Heyward, inwardly execrating the cold customs of the savages, which required such sacrifices to appearance, was fain to assume an air of indifference equal to that maintained by the chief, who was, in truth, a near relative of the afflicted woman. Just then a warrior of powerful frame darkened the door, and, stalking silently among the attentive group, he seated himself on one end of the low pile of brush that sustained Duncan. The latter cast an impatient look at his neighbour, and felt his flesh creep with uncontrollable horror when he found himself in actual contact with Magua, though undiscovered. Shrinking back in the shadow, he was relieved to hear one of the chiefs address himself to Magua, as the newest-comer.

'The Delawares have been like bears after the honeypots, prowling around my village. But who has ever found a Huron asleep?'

The darkness of the impending cloud which precedes a burst of thunder was not blacker than the brow of Magua as he exclaimed:

'The Delawares of the Lakes?'

'Not so. They who wear the petticoats of squaws on their own river. One of them has been passing the tribe.'

'Did my young men take his scalp?'

'His legs were good, though his arm is better for the hoe than the tomahawk,' returned the other, pointing to the immovable form of Uncas.

Magua stared at Uncas, then his countenance gradually lost its character of defiance in an expression of ferocious joy, and heaving a breath from the very bottom of his chest, he pronounced aloud the formidable name of—

'Le Cerf Agile!'

Each warrior sprang upon his feet at the utterance of the well-known appellation, and there was a short period during which the stoical constancy of the natives was completely conquered by surprise. The hated and yet respected name was repeated as by one voice, carrying the sound even beyond the limits of the lodge. The women and children who lingered around the entrance, took up the words in an echo, which was succeeded by another shrill and plaintive howl. The latter had not yet ended when the sensation among the men had entirely abated. Each one in presence seated himself as if ashamed of his precipitation; but it was many minutes before their eyes ceased to roll towards their captive in curious examination of a warrior who had so often proved his prowess on the best and proudest of their nation. Uncas enjoyed his victory but was content in exhibiting his triumph by a quiet smile—an emblem of scorn which belongs to all time and every nation.

Magua, caught the expression and, raising his arm, shook it at the captive, the light silver ornaments attached to his bracelet trembling with the agitation of the limb, as, in a tone of vengeance, he exclaimed in English:

'Mohican, you die!'

'The healing waters will never bring the dead Hurons to life,' returned Uncas in the music of the Delawares; 'the tumbling river washes their bones; their men are squaws; their women owls. Go—call together the Huron dogs that they may look upon a warrior. My nostrils are offended; they scent the blood of a coward'!

The latter allusion struck deep, and the injury rankled. Many of the Hurons understood the strange tongue in which the captive spoke, among which number was Magua. This cunning savage beheld, and instantly profited by his advantage. Dropping the light robe of skin from his shoulder he stretched forth his arm and commenced a burst of his dangerous and artful eloquence. He reminded them of all the Hurons who had died in the attack on the island at Glenn's and passed rapidly on to the surprise of the party by 'La Longue Carabine' and its fatal termination.

'Brothers,' he urged, 'we must not forget the dead; a redskin never ceases to remember. We will load the back of this Mohican until he staggers under our bounty, and dispatch him after my young men. Those dead warriors call on us for aid, they say, 'Forget us not.' When they see the spirit of the Mohican toiling after them with his burden, they will know we have not forgotten. I say to you, 'Let this Delaware die!'

124

The effect of such a harangue, delivered in the nervous language and the emphatic manner of a Huron orator, could scarcely be mistaken. One warrior in particular, a man of wild and ferocious mien, had been conspicuous for the attention he had given to the words of the leader. As Magua ended he arose, and, uttering the yell of a demon, his polished axe was seen glancing in the torchlight as he whirled it above his head. The motion and the cry were too sudden for words to interrupt his bloody intention. It appeared as if a bright gleam shot from his hand, which was crossed at the dark and powerful line. The former was the tomahawk in its passage; the latter the arm that Magua darted forward to divert its aim. The quick and ready motion of the chief was not entirely too late. The keen weapon cut the war-plume form the scalping tuft of Uncas and passed through the frail wall of the lodge as though it were hurled from some formidable engine.

Duncan had seen the threatening action, and sprang upon his feet with a heart which, while it leapt into his throat, swelled with the most generous resolution in behalf of his friend. A glance told him that the blow had failed, and terror changed to admiration. Uncas stood still, looking his enemy in the eye with features that seemed superior to emotion. Marble could not be colder, calmer, steadier than the countenance he put upon this sudden and vindictive attack. Then, as if pitying a want of skill that had proved so fortunate to himself, he smiled, and muttered a few words of contempt in his own tongue.

'No!' said Magua, after satisfying himself of the safety of the captive. 'The sun must shine on his shame; the squaws must see his flesh tremble, or our revenge will be like the play of boys. Go—take him where there is silence; let us see if a Delaware can sleep at night and die in the morning.'

The young men whose duty it was to guard the prisoner instantly passed their ligaments of bark across his arms and led him from the lodge, amid a profound and ominous silence. It was only as Uncas stood in the opening of the door that his firm step hesitated. There he turned and Duncan caught a look which he was glad to construe into an expression that was not entirely deserted by hope.

Magua was content with his success, or too much occupied with his secret purposes to push his inquiries any further. Shaking his mantle, and folding it on his bosom, he also quitted the place, without pursuing a subject which might have proved so fatal to the individual at his elbow. Notwithstanding his rising resentment, his natural firmness, and his anxiety on behalf of Uncas, Heyward felt sensibly relieved by the absence of so dangerous and so subtle a foe. The excitement produced by the speech gradually subsided. The warriors resumed their seats, and clouds of smoke once more filled the lodge. For near half an hour not a syllable was uttered, or scarcely a look cast aside, a grave meditative silence being in the ordinary succession to every scene of violence, and commotion amongst those beings, who were alike so impetuous and yet so self-restrained.

When the chief who had solicited the aid of Duncan finished his pipe, he made a final and successful movement towards departure, and with a motion of his finger intimated that the supposed physician was to follow. He then led Duncan away from the lodges where he had already made his unsuccessful search and proceeded directly towards the base of an adjacent mountain which overhung the temporary village. At a little distance from a bald rock and directly in its front, they entered a grassy opening which they prepared to cross. Just then a dark and mysterious-looking being arose unexpectedly in their path.

The Indian paused, as if doubtful whether to proceed, and permitted his companion to approach his side. A large black ball which at first seemed stationary, now began to move with restless and sidling attitudes that eventually conveyed to Duncan that the creature before him was a bear. Though it growled loudly and fiercely, it gave no other indications of hostility. The Huron, at least, seemed assured that the intentions of this singular intruder were peaceable, for, after giving it an attentive examination, he quietly pursued his course.

Duncan, who knew that the animal was often domesticated among the Indians, followed the example of his companion, though he was unable to prevent his eyes from looking backward, in salutary watchfulness against attacks in the rear. His uneasiness was in no way diminished when he perceived the beast rolling along their path, and following their footsteps. He would have spoken, but the Indian at that moment shoved aside a door of bark and entered a cavern in the bosom of the mountain.

Profiting by so easy a method of retreat, Duncan stepped after him, and was gladly closing the slight cover to the opening when he felt it drawn from his hand by the beast, whose shaggy form immediately darkened the passage. They were now in a straight and long gallery in a chasm of the rocks where retreat without encountering the animal was impossible. The young man pressed forward, keeping as close as possible to his conductor. The bear growled frequently at his heels, and once or twice its enormous paws were laid on his person as if disposed to prevent his farther passage into the den. Happily Duncan soon found relief as they now arrived at the place whence had proceeded the glimmer of light that had constantly been ahead.

A large cavity in the rock had been rudely fitted to answer the purposes of many apartments. The subdivisions were simple but ingenious, being composed of stone, sticks, and bark intermingled. Openings above admitted the light by day, and at night fires and torches supplied the place of the sun. Hither the Hurons had brought most of their valuables, especially those which more particularly pertained to the nation; and hither, as it now appeared, the sick woman, who was believed to be a victim of supernatural power, had been transported also, under an impression that her tormentor would find more difficulty in making his assaults through walls of stone than through the leafy coverings of the lodges. The apartment into which Duncan and his guide first entered had been exclusively devoted to her accommodation. The latter approached her bedside, which was surrounded by females, in the centre of whom Heyward was surprised to find his missing friend David.

A single look was sufficient to apprise the pretended leech that the invalid was far beyond his powers of healing. She lay in a sort of paralysis, indifferent to the objects which crowded before her sight and happily unconscious of suffering, and Heyward was thankful that his mummeries were to be performed on one who was much too ill to take interest in their success or failure.

Gamut, who had stood prepared to pour forth his spirit in song when the visitors entered, after delaying a moment, drew a strain from his pipe, and commenced a hymn that might have worked a miracle had faith in its efficacy been of much avail. He was allowed to proceed to the close, the Indians respecting his imaginary infirmity, and Duncan too glad of the delay to hazard the slightest interruption. As the dying cadence of his strains was falling on the ears of the latter, he started aside at hearing them repeated behind him in a voice half human and half sepulchral. Looking around he beheld the shaggy monster seated on end in a shadow of the cavern, where, while his restless body swung in the uneasy manner of an animal, it repeated in a sort of low growl, sounds, if not words, which bore some slight resemblance to the melody of the singer.

The effect of so strange an echo on David may be better imagined than described. His eyes opened as if he doubted the truth, and his voice became instantly mute in excess of wonder. A deep-laid scheme of communicating some important intelligence to Heywards was driven from his recollection by an emotion which very nearly resembled fear, but which he was fain to believe

128

was admiration. Under its influence he exclaimed aloud: 'She expects you, and is at hand,' and precipitately left the cavern.

There was a strange blending of the ridiculous with that which was solemn in this scene. The beast still continued its rolling and apparently untiring movements though its ludicrous attempt to imitate the melody of David ceased the instant the latter abandoned the field. The words of Gamut were, as has been seen, in his native tongue, and to Duncan they seemed pregnant with some hidden meaning, though nothing present assisted him in discovering the object of their allusions.

The chief who advanced to the bedside of the invalid beckoned away the whole group of female attendants that had clustered there to witness the skill of the stranger. He was implicitly, though reluctantly, obeyed; and when the low echo which ran along the hollow, natural gallery from the distant closing door, had ceased, pointing to his insensible daughter, he said: 'Now let my brother show his power.'

Heyward, apprehensive that the smallest delay might prove dangerous, prepared to perform that species of incantation, and those uncouth rites under which the Indian conjurors are accustomed to conceal their ignorance and impotency. His incipient attempts were interrupted by a fierce growl from the quadruped. Three separate times did he renew his efforts to proceed, and as often was he met with the same unaccountable opposition, each interruption seeming more savage and threatening than the preceding.

'The cunning ones are jealous,' said the Huron; 'I go. Brother, the woman is the wife of one of my bravest young men; deal justly by her. Peace,' he added, beckoning to the disconsolate beast to be quiet; 'I go.'

Duncan now found himself in that wild and desolate abode with the helpless invalid and the fierce and dangerous brute, which, to his utter astonishment, now seated itself before him in its natural attitude, erect like a man. Instead of uttering its discontented growls, or manifesting any further signs of anger, the whole of its shaggy body shook violently, as if agitated by some strange internal convulsion. The huge and unwieldy talons pawed stupidly about the grinning muzzle, and while Heyward kept his eyes riveted on its movements with jealous watchfulness, the grim head fell on one side and in its place appeared the honest sturdy countenance of the scout, who was indulging from the bottom of his soul in his own peculiar expression of merriment.

'Hist!' said the wary woodsman, interrupting Heyward's exclamation of surprise; 'the varlets are about the place, and any sounds that are not natural to witchcraft would bring them back upon us in a body'.

'Tell me the meaning of this masquerade, and why you have attempted so desperate an adventure!'

'Ah! Reason and calculation are often outdone by accident,' returned the scout. 'But as a story should always commence at the beginning, I will tell you the whole order. After we parted, I placed the commandant and the Sagamore in an old beaver lodge, where they are safer from the Hurons than they would be in the garrison of Edward; for your high North-West Indians, not having as yet got the traders among them, continue to venerate the beaver. After which Uncas and I pushed for the other encampment, as was agreed. Have you seen the lad?'

'To my great grief! He is captive and condemned to die at the rising of the sun.'

'I had misgivings that such would be his fate,' resumed the scout in a less confident and joyous tone. But soon regaining his naturally firm voice he continued: 'His bad fortune is the true reason for my being here, for it would never do to abandon such a boy to the Hurons. A rare time the knaves would have of it, could they tie the "Bounding Elk" and "The Long Carabine", as they call me, to the same stake!'

'Well, Uncas and I fell in with a return party of the varlets; the lad was much too forward for a scout; nay, for that matter, being of hot blood, he was not much to blame; and after all, one of the Hurons proved a coward, and in fleeing led him into an ambushment.

'After the loss of the boy I turned upon the Hurons, as you may judge. There have been scrimmages atween one or two of their outliers and myself; but that is neither here nor there. So after I had shot the imps, I got in pretty nigh to the lodges without further commotion. Then what should luck do in my favour but lead me to the very spot where one of the most famous conjurors of the tribe was dressing himself, as I well knew, for some great battle with Satan, though why should I call that luck which it now seems was an especial ordering of Providence. So a judgmatical rap over the head stiffened the lying impostor for a time, and leaving him a bit of walnut for his supper to prevent an uproar, and stringing him up atween two saplings, I made free with his finery, and took the part of the bear on myself, in order that the operations might proceed. But all our work is yet before us: where is the gentle one?'

'Heaven knows! I have examined every lodge in the village without discovering the slightest trace of her presence in the tribe.'

'You heard what the singer said as he left us: "She is at hand and expects you."'

'I have been compelled to believe he alluded to the sick woman.'

'The simpleton was frightened and blundered through his message, but he had a deeper meaning. Here are walls enough to separate the whole settlement. A bear ought to climb, therefore I will look above them; there may be honey pots hid in these rocks.'

The scout clambered up the partition, but the instant the summit was gained he made a gesture for silence, and slid down with the utmost precipitation.

'She is here', he whispered, 'and by that door you will find her. Go by that passage there and find a way round.'

Duncan had no other guide than a distant glimmering light which served, however, the office of a polar star to the lover. By its aid he was able to enter the haven of his hopes, which was merely another apartment in the cavern that had been solely appropriated to the safe-keeping of so important a prisoner as the daughter of the commandant of William Henry. It was profusely strewed with the plunder of that unlucky fortress. In the midst of this confusion he found her he sought, pale, anxious and terrified, but lovely. David had prepared her for such a visit.

'Duncan!' she exclaimed, in a voice that seemed to tremble at the sounds created by itself.

'Alice!' he answered, leaping carelessly amongtrunks, boxes, arms and furniture until he stood at her side.

'I knew that you would never desert me,' she said looking up with a momentary glow on her otherwise dejected countenance. 'And dearest Cora, Duncan; surely Cora was not forgotten?'

'Not forgotten, no! Regretted as woman was seldom mourned before. Your venerable father knew no difference between his children; but I—Alice, you will not be offended when I say that to me her worth was in a degree obscured ...'

'Then you knew not the merit of my sister,' said Alice withdrawing her hand. 'Of you she ever speaks as of one who is her dearest friend.'

'I would gladly believe her such,' returned Duncan hastily; 'I could wish her to be even more; but with you, Alice, I have the permission of your father to aspire to a still nearer and dearer tie.'

Alice trembled violently, and there was an instant during which she bent her face aside, yielding to the emotions common to her sex; but they quickly passed away leaving her mistress of her deportment, if not her affections.

'Heyward,' she said, looking him full in the face with a touching expression of innocence and dependency, 'give me the sacred presence and the holy sanction of that parent before you urge me further.'

'Though more I should not, less I could not say', the youth was about to answer, when he was interrupted by a light tap on the shoulder. Starting to his feet he turned, and, confronting the intruder, his looks fell on the dark and malignant visage of Magua. The deep gutteral laugh of the savage sounded at such a moment to Duncan like the hellish taunt of a demon, and believing himself irretrievably lost, he drew Alice to his bosom and stood prepared to meet his fate.

But Magua meditated no immediate violence. He dropped a log of wood across a door different from that by which Duncan had entered nor did he ever bestow a second glance at the motionless embracing forms in the centre of the cavern until he had completely cut off every hope of retreat through the private outlet he had himself used. When Magua had effected his object, he approached his prisoners and said in English:

'The pale-faces trap the cunning beavers, but the redskins know how to take the Yengeese.'

'Huron, do your worst,' exclaimed the excited Heyward, forgetful that a double stake was involved in his life. 'You and your vengeance are alike despised.'

'Will the white man speak these words at the stake?' asked Magua, manifesting at the same time how little faith he had in the other's resolution by the sneer that accompanied his words.

'Here, singly to your face, or in the presence of your nation.'

'Le Renard Subtil is a great chief,' returned the Indian. 'He will go and bring his young men to see how bravely a pale-face can laugh at the tortures.'

He turned away while speaking, and was about to leave the place through the avenue by which Duncan had approached when a growl caught his ear. The figure of the bear appeared in the door where it sat, rolling from side to side with its customary recklessness. Magua eyed it keenly for a moment, as if to ascertain its character. Then, so soon as he recognized the well-known attire of the conjuror, he prepared to pass it in cool contempt, and moved resolutely forward.

'Fool!' exclaimed the chief in Huron, 'Go play with the children and squaws; leave men to their wisdom.'

He once more endeavoured to pass the supposed empiric, scorning even the parade of threatening to use the knife or tomahawk that was pendant from his belt. Suddenly the beast extended its arms, or rather legs, and enclosed him in a grasp that might have vied with the far-famed power of the 'bear's hug' itself. Heyward, who had breathlessly watched the whole procedure on the part of Hawk-eye, now caught up a thong of buckskin which had been used around some bundle, and when he beheld his enemy with two arms pinned to his side by the iron muscles of the scout, he rushed upon him and effectually secured arms, legs and feet in twenty folds of the thong. When the formidable Huron was completely pinioned, the scout released his hold, and Duncan, laid his enemy on his back, utterly helpless.

Throughout the whole of this sudden and extraordinary operation, Magua, though he had struggled violently until assured he was in the hands of one whose nerves were far better than his own, had not uttered the slightest exclamation. But when Hawk-eye by way of making a summary explanation of his conduct removed the shaggy jaws of the beast, and exposed his own rugged and earnest countenance to the gaze of the Huron, the philosophy of the latter was so far mastered as to permit him to utter the never-failing:

'Hugh!'

'Ay, you've found your tongue,' said the undisturbed conqueror. 'Now, that you shall not use it to our ruin, I must make free to stop your mouth.'

As there was no time to be lost, the scout immediately set about effecting so necessary a precaution; and when he had gagged the Indian, his enemy might safely have been considered hors de combat.

'Quick! We must make a push for the woods,' said the industrious scout when his work was ended. 'The very helplessness of the maiden lying there insensible can help us. Wrap her in them Indian cloths. Take her in your arms and follow.'

Obediently Duncan took her light person in his arms and followed on the footsteps of the scout. They found the sick woman as they had left her, still alone, and passed swiftly on by the natural gallery to the place of entrance. As they approached the little door of bark, a murmur of voices without announced that the friends and relatives of the invalid were gathered about the place, patiently awaiting a summons to re-enter.

'If I open my lips to speak,' Hawk-eye whispered, 'my English which is the genuine tongue of a white skin, will tell the varlets than an enemy is among them. You must give 'em your jargon, Major, and say that we have shut the evil spirit in the cave and are taking the woman to the woods in order to find strengthening roots. Practise all your cunning, for it is a lawful undertaking.'

The scout boldly threw open the covering of bark and left the place, enacting the character of the bear as he proceeded. Duncan kept close at his heels, and soon found himself in the centre of a cluster of twenty anxious relatives and friends.

The crowd fell back a little, and permitted the father, and one who appeared to be the husband of the woman, to approach.

'Has my brother driven away the evil spirit?' demanded the former. 'What has he in his arms?'

'Thy child,' returned Duncan gravely; 'the disease has gone out of her; it is shut in the rocks. I take the woman to a distance where I will strengthen her against any further attacks. She shall be in the wigwam of the young man when the sun comes again.'

When the father had translated the meaning of the stranger's words into the Huron language, a suppressed murmur expressed the satisfaction with which this intelligence was received. The chief himself waved his hand for Duncan to proceed, saying aloud in a firm voice and in a lofty manner:

'Go! I am a man, and I will enter the rock and fight the wicked one.'

Heyward stopped short in dismay, remembering the bound body of Magua.

'Is my brother mad?' he exclaimed. 'Is he cruel? He will meet the disease and it will enter him; or he will drive out the disease and it will chase his daughter into the woods. No; let my children wait without, and if the spirit appears, beat him down with clubs. He is cunning, and will bury himself in the mountain when he sees how many are ready to fight him.'

This singular warning had the desired effect. The father and the husband, instead of entering, posted themselves at the entrance in readiness to deal their vengeance on the imaginary tormentor of their sick relative, and at this favourable moment the counterfeit conjurors' disappeared.

Hawk-eye, at the same time that he had presumed on the nature of the Indian superstitions, was not ignorant that they were rather tolerated than relied on by the wisest of the chiefs. He well knew the value of time in the present emergency. Taking the path, therefore, th t was most likely to avoid observation, he rather skirted than entered the village.

Alice had revived under the renovating influence of the open air, and as her physical rather than her mental powers had been the subject of weakness, she stood in no need of any explanation of that which had occurred.

'Now let me make an effort to walk,' she said when they had entered the forest, blushing, though unseen, that she had not been sooner able to quit the arms of Duncan. 'I an indeed restored.'

'Nay, Alice, you are yet too weak.'

The maiden struggled gently to release herself, and Heyward was compelled' to part with his precious burden. When the scout found himself a suitable distance from the lodges, he made a halt and spoke on a subject of which he was thoroughly the master.

'This path will lead you to a brook,' he said. 'Follow its northern bank until you come to a fall; mount the hill on your right, and you will see the fires of the other people. There you must go and demand protection; if they are true Delawares you will be safe. A distant flight with that gentle one just now is impossible. The Hurons would follow up our trail and master our scalps before we had got a dozen miles. Go, and Providence be with you!'

'And you?' demanded Heyward in surprise. 'Surely we part not here?'

'The Hurons hold the pride of the Delawares; the last of the high blood of the Mohicans is in their power,' returned the scout. 'I go to see what can be done in his favour. Had they mastered your scalp, Major, a knave should have fallen for every hair it held, as I promised; but if the young Sagamore is to be led to the stake, the Indians shall see also how a man without a cross can die.'

Not in the least offended with the decided preferences that the sturdy woodsman gave to one who might, in some degree, be called the child of his adoption, Duncan still continued to urge such reasons against so desperate an effort as presented themselves. He was aided by Alice but their eloquence and ingenuity were expended in vain.

It was of no avail and in the end Duncan released his hold on the arm of the scout, who turned and steadily retraced his steps towards the lodges. After pausing a moment to gaze at his retiring form, the successful and yet sorrowful Heyward, and Alice, took their way together towards the distant village of the Delawares.

AT THE MERCY OF THE DELAWARES

During his return to the camp, Hawk-eye's steps became more deliberate and his vigilant eye suffered no sign, whether friendly or hostile, to escape him. A neglected hut was a little in advance of the others, and appeared as if it had been deserted. A faint light glimmered through its cracks and announced that, notwithstanding its imperfect structure, it was not without a tenant. Thither, then, the scout proceeded, crawling to a little opening where he might command a view of the interior. It proved to be the abiding place of David Gamut. Hither the faithful singing-master had now brought himself, together with all his sorrows and apprehensions.

Hawk-eye, first making a circuit of the hut and ascertaining that it stood quite alone ventured through its low door into the very presence of Gamut. The suddenness and the nature of the surprise nearly proved too much for—we will not say the philosophy—but for the fait and resolution of David. He fumbled with his pitch-pipe and arose with a confused intention of attempting a musical exorcism.

The bear shook his shaggy sides, and then a well-known voice spoke:

'Put up the tootin' we'pon, and teach your throat modesty. Five words of comprehendable English are worth, just now, an hour of squalling.'

'What art thou?' demanded David, utterly disqualified to pursue his original intention, and nearly gasping for breath.

'A man like yourself and one whose blood is as little tainted by the cross of a bear, or an Indian, as your own. Have you so soon forgotten from whom you

received the foolish instrument you hold in your hand?'
returned Hawk-eye, uncasing his honest countenance,
the better to assure the wavering confidence of his
companion.

'Can these things be?' gasped David, as the truth
began to dawn upon him. 'First tell me then of the
maiden and of the youth who so bravely sought her.'

'Ay, they are happily freed from the tomahawks of
these varlets. But can you put me on the scent of
Uncas?'

'The young man is in bondage and much I fear his
death is decreed.'

'Can you lead me to him?'

'The task will not be difficult,' returned David, hesit-
ating; 'though I greatly fear your presence would
rather increase than mitigate his unhappy fortunes.'

'No more words, but lead on,' returned Hawk-eye,
concealing his face again, and setting the example in
his own person by instantly quitting the lodge.

As they proceeded, the scout ascertained that his
companion found access to Uncas under privilege of his
imagined infirmity, aided by the favour he had ac-
quired with one of the guards, who, in consequence
of speaking a little English, had been selected by David
as the subject of a religious conversion.

The lodge in which Uncas was confined was in the
very centre of the village, and in a situation perhaps
more difficult than any other to approach or leave
without observation. But it was not the policy of
Hawk-eye to effect the least concealment. Presuming,
on his disguise and his ability to sustain the character
he had assumed, he took the most plain and direct
route to the place.

Four or five of the warriors only lingered about the
door of the prison of Uncas, wary but close observers
of the manner of their captive. At the sight of Gamut
accompanied by one in the well-known masquerade of
their most distinguished conjuror, they readily made
way for them both, though they betrayed no intention
to depart themselves.

139

From the total inability of the scout to address the Hurons in their own language, he was compelled to trust the conversation entirely to David. Notwithstanding the simplicity of the latter he did ample justice to the instructions he had received, more than fulfilling the strongest hopes of his teacher.

'The Delawares are women!' he exclaimed addressing himself to the savage who had a slight understanding of the language in which he spoke. 'The Yengeese, my foolish countrymen, have told them to take up the tomahawk, and strike their fathers in the Canadas, and they have forgotten their sex. Does my brother wish to hear "Le Cerf Agile" ask for his pettitcoats, and see him weep before the Hurons at the stake?'

The exclamation 'Hugh!' delivered in a strong tone of assent, announced the gratification the savages would receive in witnessing such an exhibition of weakness in an enemy so long hated and so much feared.

'Then let him step aside, and the cunning man will blow upon the dog! Tell it to my brothers.'

The Huron explained the meaning of David to his followers, who, greatly gratified at the prospect of such a refinement of cruelty, motioned the supposed conjuror to enter.

But the bear, instead of obeying, maintained the seat it had taken and growled.

'The cunning man is afraid his breath will blow upon his brothers, and take away their courage too,' continued David, improved the hint he received. 'They must stand farther off.'

The Hurons who would have deemed such a misfortune the heaviest calamity that could befall them, fell back in a body, taking a position where they were out of earshot, though at the same time they could command a view of the entrance to the lodge. Then, as if satisfied of their safety, the scout slowly left his position and slowly entered the place.

Uncas occupied a distant corner, in a reclining attitude, being rigidly bound, both hands and feet, by strong and painful withes. When the frightful object first presented itself to the young Mohican, he did not deign to bestow a single glance on the animal. As soon, however, as a low hissing sound like that of a serpent was heard proceeding from the mouth of the beast in place of the fierce growling of the bear, Uncas uttered in a deep, suppressed voice:

'Hawk-eye!'

'Cut his bonds,' said Hawk-eye to David, who just then approached them.

The singer did as he was ordered, and Uncas found his limbs released, though he allowed neither tongue nor feature to betray any symptom of surprise. A moment later Hawk-eye had cast his shaggy bear-skin vestment, which was done simply by loosening certain thongs of skin, and drawing a long, glittering knife, put it in the hands of Uncas.

'The red Hurons are without,' he said. 'Let us be ready.'

'We will go,' said Uncas.

'Whither?'

'To the Tortoises, they are the children of my grandfathers.'

'Ay, but what shall we do with the Mingoes at the door? They count six, and this singer is as good as nothing.'

'The Hurons run like snails,' said Uncas scornfully. 'The Delawares are children of the tortoise, and they outstrip the deer.'

'I doubt not, on a rush, you would pass the whole nation, but as for myself, while I can brain a Huron as well as a better man, when it comes to a race the knaves would prove too much for me. Still, what can't be done by main courage in war must be done by circumvention. Put on the bear-skin here; I doubt not you can play the bear nearly as well as myself.'

Silently and expeditiously Uncas encased himself in the covering of the beast.

'Now, friend,' said Hawk-eye, addressing David, 'an exchange of garment between us will also be a great convenience. Take my hunting-shirt and cap, and give me your blanket and hat. You must trust me, too, with the book and spectacles, as well as the tooter. You shall have all back again, if we meet in better times.'

When Hawk-eye's restless eyes were hid behind the glasses, and his head surmounted by the triangular beaver, as their statures were not dissimilar, he might readily have passed for the singer by starlight.

He now gave parting instructions to David who had meantime donned Hawk-eye's shirt and cap.

'Your chiefest danger will be at the moment when the savages find out they have been deceived. You must sit down here in the shadows and take the part of Uncas until such time as the Indians discover the cheat, when your time of trial will come. Meantime, hold your head down, and draw in your legs. Keep silent as long as may be; and it would be wise, when you do speak, to break our suddenly in one of your shoutings, which will serve to remind the Indians that you are not altogether responsible as man should be. God bless you friend.'

So saying the scout shook David cordially by the hand and immediately left the lodge attended by the new representative of the beast.

The instant Hawk-eye found himself under the observation of the Hurons, he drew up his tall form in the rigid manner of David, threw out his arm in the act of keeping time, and commenced what he intended for an imitation of his psalmody. When at the nearest point to the dark group of savages, the Huron who spoke the English thrust out an arm, and stopped the supposed singing master.

'The Delaware dog,' he said, leaning forward and peering through the dim light to catch the expression of the other's features, 'is he afraid? Will the Hurons hear his groans?'

At this question, a growl so exceedingly fierce and natural proceeded from the beast which followed the singing-master that the young Indian released his hold and started aside as if to assure himself that it was not a veritable bear, and no counterfeit, that was rolling before him. Hawk-eye profited from this interruption to break out into a burst of musical expression, and the Indians drew back in a body, and suffered, as they thought, the conjuror and his inspired assistant to proceed.

The adventurers had got clear of the village, and were now swiftly approaching the shelter of the woods, when a loud and long cry arose from the lodge where Uncas had been confined. The next instant a burst of cries filled the outer air, and ran along the whole extent of the village. Uncas cast his skin, and stepped forth in his own magnificent proportions. Hawk-eye tapped him lightly on the shoulder and glided ahead.

'Now let the devils strike our scent!' said the scout tearing two rifles, with all their attendant accoutrements, from beneath a bush and flourishing 'Kill-deer' as he handed Uncas his weapon; 'two, at least, will find it to their deaths.'

Then, throwing their pieces to a low trail, like sportsmen in readiness for their game, they dashed forward, and were soon buried in the sombre darkness of the forest.

The impatience of the savages who lingered about the prison of Uncas, as has been seen, had overcome their dread of the conjuror's breath. They stole cautiously and with beating hearts to a crevice through which the faint light of the fire was glimmering. For several minutes they mistook the form of David for that of their prisoner but the very accident which Hawk-eye had foreseen occurred. The singer gradually suffered his lower limbs to extend themselves, and then turned his head so that his face could be seen by those outside. With a cry the natives rushed together into the lodge and laying their hands with but little ceremony on their captive immediately detected the imposition. Then arose the cry first heard by the fugitives. It was succeeded by the most frantic and angry demonstrations of vengeance. David was fain to trust to a memory that rarely failed him on such subjects, and breaking forth in a loud and impassioned strain, he endeavoured to smooth his passage into the other world by singing the opening verse of a funeral anthem. The Indians were seasonably reminded of his infirmity and rushing into the open air they aroused the village in the manner described. The escape was soon known and the whole tribe crowded in a body around the council lodge, all looking round in wonder that Magua did not appear amid the other chiefs. Messengers were dispatched to his lodge requiring his presence; in the meantime some of the swiftest young men were ordered to make the circuit of the clearing under cover of the woods, in order to ascertain that their suspected neighbours, the Delawares, designed no mischief.

The clamour of many voices soon announced that a party approached, who might be expected to communicate some intelligence that would explain the mystery of the novel surprise. The crowd without gave way, and several warriors entered the place, bringing with them the hapless conjuror who, stripped of his bear disguise by Hawk-eye, had been so long left by the scout in duress.

Notwithstanding this man was held in very unequal estimation among the Hurons, some believing implicitly in his power, and others deeming him an impostor, he was now listened to by all with the deepest attention. When his brief story was ended, the father of the sick woman stepped forth, and in a few pithy expressions, related in his turn what he knew of a bear conjuror. These two narratives gave a proper direction to the subsequent inquiries, which were now made with the characteristic cunning of savages.

Ten of the wisest and firmest among the chiefs were selected for the purpose and now made their way to the cavern. The outer apartment was silent and gloomy. The woman lay in her usual place and posture, though there were those present who affirmed they had seen her borne to the wood by the supposed 'medicine of the white men'. Chafed by the silent imputation and inwardly troubled by so unaccountable a circumstance, the chief advanced to the side of the bed, and, stooping, cast an incredulous look at the features, as if distrusting their reality. His daughter was dead!

'The wife of my young man has left us! The Great Spirit is angry with his children,' he declared.

The mournful intelligence was received in solemn silence. After a short pause one of the elder Indians was about to speak, when a dark looking object was seen rolling out of an adjoining apartment into the very centre of the room where they stood. Ignorant of the nature of the beings they had to deal with, the whole party drew back a little and gazed in admiration, until the object fronted the light, and, rising on end, exhibited the distorted but still fierce and sullen features of Magua. The discovery was succeded by a general exclamation of amazement.

As soon, however, as the true situation of the chief was understood, several ready knives appeared and his limbs and tongue were quickly released. The Huron arose and shook himself like a lion quitting his lair. Not a word escaped him, though his hand played convulsively with the handle of his knife, while his lowering eyes scanned the whole party, as if they sought an object suited to the first burst of his vengeance. Meeting everywhere faces that he knew as friends the savage grated his teeth and swallowed his passion for want of a victim on whom to vent it. Several minutes, passed thus before the oldest of the party spoke.

'My friend has found an enemy,' he said. 'Is he nigh, that the Hurons may take revenge?'

'Let the Delaware die!' exclaimed Magua in a voice of thunder.

Another long and expressive silence was observed, and was broken as before, with due precaution, by the same individual.

'The Mohican is swift of foot, and leaps far,' he said, 'but my young men are on his trail.'

'Is he gone?' demanded Magua in tones so deep and guttural that they seemed to proceed from his inmost chest.

'An evil spirit has been among us, and the Delaware has blinded our eyes.'

'An evil spirit!' repated the other mockingly. "Tis the spirit of the dog who carries the heart and cunning of a Huron under a pale skin—La Longue Carabine.'

The pronunciation of so terrible a name produced the usual effect among his auditors. Some among them gnashed their teeth in anger, others vented their feelings in yells, and some again beat the air frantically as if the object of their resentment were suffering under their blows. When this sudden outbreak of temper subsided into still and sullen restraint, Magua too changed his manner, and assumed the air of one who knew how to think and act with a dignity worthy of so grave a subject.

'Let us go to my people,' he said; 'they wait for us.

His companions consented in silence, and the whole of the party left the cavern and returned to the council lodge. When they were seated, all eyes turned on Magua, who understood from such an indication, that by common consent they had devolved the duty of relating what had passed on him. He arose and told his tale without duplicity or reservation. The next considera‐ tion now, was the means and oppotunities for revenge.

Additional pursuers had already been sent on the trail of the fugitives and when some of the runners returned with the report that it was in the neighbour‐ ing camp of the Delawares, their suspected allies, that the runaways had taken refuge, several of the chiefs proposed deep and dangerous schemes to surprise that tribe, gain possession of their camp, and recover their prisoners by the same blow.

Magua had other ideas. In obedience to the invariable rule of Indian policy, the sisters had been separated as soon as they reached the Huron camp. Because Magua knew that in retaining the person of Alice, he possessed the most effectual check on Cora, he had therefore kept the former within reach and consigned the one he most valued to the keeping of their allies. The arrangement was understood to be merely temporary and Magua knew that Indian policy should ensure her safe return to him without fighting. These thoughts, however, he kept to himself, but by skilful use of oratory, he now won over the Hurons to act, with deliberation and moderation, trusting the direction of the whole affair to the government of the chief who suggested such wise and intelligible expedients.

Magua had now attained the one great object of all his cunning and enterprise. He was, in truth, their ruler; and so long as he could maintain his popularity, no monarch could be more despotic, especially while the tribe continued in a hostile country. Throwing off, therefore, the appearance of consultation, he assumed the grave air necessary to support the dignity of his office.

Runners were dispatched for intelligence in different directions; spies were ordered to approach and feel the encampment of the Delawares; the warriors were dismissed to their lodges, with an intimation that their services would soon be needed; and the women and children were ordered to retire, with a warning that it was their province to be silent. When these several arrangements were made, Magua passed through the village, stopping here and there to pay a visit where he thought his presence might be flattering to the individual. Then he sought his own lodge.

Long before the day dawned, however, warrior after warrior entered the solitary hut of Magua, until they had collected to the number of twenty. Each bore his rifle and all the other accoutrements of war, though the paint was uniformly peaceful.

Then Magua arose and gave the signal to proceed, marching himself in silence. They followed their leader singly and in that well-known order which has obtained the distinguishing appelation of 'Indian file'. Unlike other men engaged in the spirit-stirring business of war, they stole from their camp unostentatiously and unobserved.

Instead of taking the path which led directly to the camp of the Delawares, Magua led his party for some distance down the windings of the stream and along the little artificial lake of the beavers. The day began to dawn as they entered the clearing which had been formed by those sagacious and industrious animals. Though Magua, who had resumed his ancient garb, bore the outline of a fox on the dressed skin which formed his robe, there was one chief of his party who carried the beaver as his peculiar symbol or 'totem'. There would have been a species of profanity in the mission, had this man passed so powerful a community of his fancied kindred without bestowing some evidence of his regard. Accordingly at the beaver pool he paused and spoke to the animals as if he were addressing more intelligent beings. Just as he ended his addres, the head of a large beaver was thrust from the door of a dilapidated and uninhabited lodge. Such an extraordinary sign of confidence was received by the orator as a highly favourable omen before they again moved off at a signal from Magua.

Had any of the Hurons turned to look behind them, they would have seen the animal watching their movement with an interest and sagacity that might easily have been mistaken for reason. Indeed, so very distinct and intelligible were the devices of the quadruped, that even the most experienced observer would have been at a loss to account for its actions, until the moment when the party entered the forest, when the whole would have been explained by seeing the entire animal issue from the lodge, uncasing, by the act, the grave features of Chingachgook from his mask of fur.

The tribe, or rather half-tribe, of Delawares which has been so often mentioned, and whose present place of encampment was so nigh the temporary village of the Hurons, could assemble about an equal number of warriors with the latter people. Like their neighbours they had followed Montcalm into the territories of the English crown, and were making heavy and serious inroads on the hunting grounds of the Mohawks; though they had seen fit, with the mysterious reserve so common among the natives, to withold their assistance at

148

the moment when it was most required. The French had accounted for this unexpected defection on the part of their ally in various ways. It was the prevalent opinion, however, that they had been influenced by veneration for the ancient treaty that had once made them dependent on the Six Nations for military protection, and now rendered them reluctant to encounter their former masters. As for the tribe itself, it had been content to announce to Montcalm through his emissaries, with Indian brevity, that their hatchets were dull, and time was necessary to sharpen them. The politic captain of the Canadas had deemed it wiser to submit to entertain a passive friend than by any acts of ill-judged severity to convert him into an open enemy.

On that morning when Magua led his silent party from the settlements of the beavers into the forest, in the manner described, the sun rose upon the Delaware encampment as if it had suddenly burst upon a busy people actively employed in all the customary avocations of high noon. The women ran from lodge to lodge, bent on seeking the comforts necessary to their habits. The warriors were lounging in groups, speaking like men who deeply weighed their opinions; the instruments of the chase were to be seen in abundance among the lodges, but none departed; and occasionally the eyes of a whole group were turned simultaneously towards a large and silent lodge in the centre of the village as if it contained the subject of their common thoughts.

During the existence of this scene, a man suddenly appeared at the farthest extremity of a platform of rock which formed the level of the village. He was without arms and his paint tended rather to soften than increase the natural sternness of his austere countenance. When in full view of the Delawares he stopped, and made a gesture of amity by throwing his arm upwards towards heaven, and then letting if fall impressively on his breast. The inhabitants of the village answered his salute by a low murmur of welcome and encouraged him to advance by similar indications of friendship. When he had reached the group in which it was evident that the principal chiefs were collected, the stranger paused. Then the Delawares saw that the active and erect form that stood before them was that of the well-known Huron chief, Le Renard Subtil. His reception was grave, silent and wary. The warriors in front stepped aside, opening their way to their most approved orator by the action, one who spoke all those languages that were cultivated among the northern aborigines.

'The wise Huron is welcome,' said the Delaware in the language of the Maquas. 'He is come to eat his "succatash" with his brothers of the lakes.'

'He is come,' repeated Magua, bending his head with the dignity of an Eastern prince.

The chief extended his arm, and, taking the other by the wrist they once more exchanged friendly salutations. Then the Delaware invited his guest to enter his own lodge and share his morning meal. When the appetites of the two were appeased, the squaws removed the trenchers and gourds, and the two parties began to prepare themselves for a subtle trial of their wits.

'Is the face of my great Canada father turned again towards his Huron Children?' demanded the orator of the Delawares.

'He calls them most beloved,' returned Magua.

The Delaware gravely bowed his acquiescence to what he knew to be false. Then Magua demanded:

'Does my prisoner give trouble to my brothers?'

'She is welcome.'

'The path between the Hurons and the Delawares is short; let her be sent to my squaws if she gives trouble to my brother.'

'She is welcome' replied the Delaware chief more emphatically.

Magua continued silent several minutes, baffled by the repulse he had received in this his opening effort to regain possession of Cora. Then he tried another course.

150

'Have there not been strange moccasins in the woods? Have not my brothers scented the feet of white men?'

'Let my Canada father come,' returned the other evasively. 'His children are ready to see him.'

Magua now shifted his ground when he found himself unable to penetrate the caution of his opponent.

'I have brought gifts to my brother. Behold!' And gravely he spread his presents before the dazzled eyes of his hosts. This well-judged and politic stroke was not without instantaneous results. The Delawares lost their gravity and the host himself repeated with strong emphasis the words:

'My brother is a wise chief. He is welcome.'

'The Hurons love their friends the Delawares,' returned Magua. 'The redskins should be friends and look with open eyes on the white man. Has not my brother scented spies in the woods?'

The Delaware's countenance grew less stern, and he now deigned to answer more directly.

'There have been strange moccasins about my camp. They have been tracked into my lodges.'

'Did my brother beat out the dogs?' asked Magua.

'It would not do. The stranger is always welcome to the children of the Lenape.'

'The stranger but not the spy. What will the Canada father think when he hears that his greatest enemy is fed in the camp of his children? When he is told a bloody Yengee smokes at your fire? That the pale-face who has slain so many of his friends goes in and out among the Delawares?'

'Where is the Yengee that the Delawares fear?' returned the other. 'Who is the mortal enemy of my Great Father?'

'La Longue Carabine!'

The Delaware warriors started at the well-known name.

'What does my brother mean?' demanded their speaker in a tone of amazement.

'Let the Delawares count their prisoners,' returned Magua coldly. 'They will find one whose skin is neither red nor pale.'

A long and musing pause succeeded. The chief consulted apart with his companions, and messengers were dispatched to collect certain others of the most distinguished men of the tribe.

As warrior after warrior dropped in, they were each made acquainted in turn with the important intelligence that Magua had communicated. The air of surprise and the usual low, deep guttural exclamation were common to them all. The news spread from mouth to mouth, until the whole encampment became powerfully agitated. When the excitement had a little abated, the old men disposed themselves seriously to consider that which it became the honour and safety of their tribe to perform, under circumstances of so much delicacy and embarassment.

The council of the Delawares was short. When it was ended a general bustle announced that it was to be immediately succeeded by a solemn and formal assemblage of the nation, and within half an hour each individual was in his place, to a number exceeding a thousand souls. It rested solely with the oldest and most experienced of the men to lay the subject of the conference before the people.

At length, one of those low murmurs that are so apt to disturb a multitude was heard, and the whole nation arose to their feet by a common impulse. At that instant the door of the lodge to which their glances had strayed, opened, and three men slowly approached the place of consultation. They were all aged, even beyond that period to which the oldest present had reached; but one in the centre, who leaned on his companions for support, had numbered an amount of years to which the human race is seldom permitted to attain. His form, which had once been tall and erect as the cedar, was now bending under the pressure of more than a century. The elastic light step of an Indian was gone, and in its place he was compelled to toil his tardy way over the ground inch by inch.

So soon as the first hum of emotion and pleasure, which the sudden appearance of this venerated individual created, had a little subsided, the name of 'Tamenund' was whispered from mouth to mouth. Magua had often heard the fame of this wise and just Delaware, a reputation that even proceeded so far as to bestow on him the rare gift of holding secret communication with the Great Spirit.

The eyes of the old man were closed, as though the organs were wearied with having so long witnessed the selfish workings of the human passions. Notwithstanding the position of the Huron, he passed the observant and silent Magua without notice, and leaning on his two venerable supporters, proceeded to the high place of the multitude where he seated himself in the centre of his nation with the dignity of a monarch and the air of a father.

After a short delay, a few of the young men, to whom instructions had been whispered by one of the aged attendants of Tamenund, arose, left the crowd and entered the lodge which has already been noted as the object of so much attention throughout the morning. In a few minutes they reappeared, escorting the individuals who had caused all these solemn preparations towards the seat of judgement. The crowd opened in a lane, and when the party had reentered, it closed in again, forming a large and dense belt of human bodies arranged in an open circle.

10

TRIAL BY A PATRIARCH

Cora stood foremost amongst the prisoners, entwining her arms in those of Alice in the tenderness of sisterly love. Notwithstanding the fearful and menacing array of savages on every side of her, no apprehension on her own account could prevent the noble-minded maiden from keeping her eyes fastened on the pale and anxious features of the trembling Alice. Close at her side stood Heyward, with an interest in both that at such a moment of intense uncertainty scarcely knew a preponderance in favour of her whom he most loved. Hawkeye had placed himself a little in the rear, with a deference to the superior rank of his companions that no similarity in the state of their present fortunes could induce him to forget. Uncas was not there.

When perfect silence was again restored, and after the usual long, impressive pause, one of the two aged chiefs who sat at the side of the patriarch arose and demanded aloud, in very intelligible English:

'Which of my prisoners is "La Longue Carabine"?'

At once both Duncan and the scout claimed the privilege. They saw immediately that this wily savage had some secret purpose in their present summons before the nation and had determined to throw every possible impediment in the way of the execution of his sinister plans. At last, however, the sagacity of the Indians extracted the real merits of the point in controversy and effectually established Hawk-eye in the possession of his dangerous reputation. He immediately became the principal object of attention to those around. Only when their sudden and noisy commotion died the aged chief turned his eyes on Magua.

'Now, brother, speak. The Delawares listen.'

Thus singled and directly called to declare his object, the Huron arose and placed himself in an attitude to speak. On Hawk-eye he cast a glance of respectful enmity, on Duncan a look of extinguished hatred, the shrinking figure of Alice he scarcely deigned to notice, but when his glance met the firm, commanding and yet lovely form of Cora, his eye lingered long. Then, filled with his own dark intentions, he spoke in the language of the Canadas.

'The Spirit that made men coloured them differently. Some are blacker than the sluggish bear; these he said should be slaves. Some he made with faces paler than the ermine of the forests; these he ordered to be traders with appetites to devour the earth. Such are the pale-faces, to whom God gave enough and yet he wants all.

'Some the Great Spirit made with skins brighter and redder than yonder sun. They were brave; they were just; they were happy. Some he placed among the snows, some near the setting sun, some on the lands around the great fresh waters: but to his greatest and most beloved he gave the sands of the salt lake. Do my brothers know the name of this favoured people?'

'It was the Lenape!' exclaimed twenty eager voices in a breath.

'It was the Lenni Lenape,' returned Magua. 'But why should a Huron of the woods tell a wise people of their traditions? Why remind them of their injuries, their losses, their defeats, their misery ? I have done. My tongue is still, for my heart is of lead.'

As the voice of the speaker suddenly ceased, every face and all eyes turned by a common movement towards the venerable Tamenund. From the moment he took his seat till the present instant the lips of the patriarch had not severed, and scarcely a sign of life had escaped him. At the nicely graduated sounds of Magua's voice, however, he betrayed some evidence of consciousness, and once or twice he even raised his head as if to listen. But when the crafty Huron spoke of his nation by name, the eyelids of the old man raised themselves, and he looked out upon the multitude with that sort of dull unmeaning expression which might be supposed to belong to the countenance of a spectre. Then he made an effort to rise, and, being upheld by his supporters, he gained his feet in a posture commanding by its dignity, while he tottered with weakness.

'Who calls upon the children of the Lenape?' he said in a deep guttural voice that was rendered awfully audible by the breathless silence of the multitude. 'Who speaks of things gone?'

'It is a Wyandot,' said Magua, stepping nigher to the rude platform on which the other stood, 'a friend of Tamenund.'

'A friend!' repeated the sage, on whose brow a dark frown settled, imparting a portion of that severity which had rendered his eye so terrible in middle age. 'Are the Mingoes rulers of the earth? What brings a Huron here?'

'Justice. His prisoners are with his brothers and he comes for his own.'

Tamenund turned his head towards one of this supporters, and listened to the short explanation the man gave. Then, facing the applicant, he regarded him a moment with deep attention, after which he said in a low and reluctant voice:

'Justice is the law of the great Manitto. My children, give the stranger food. Then, Huron, take thine own and depart.'

On the delivery of this solemn judgement the patriarch seated himself and closed his eyes again, as if better pleased with the images of his own ripened experience than with the visible objects of the world.

Against such a decree there was no Delaware sufficiently hardy to murmur. Magua cast a look of triumph around the whole assembly before he proceeded to the execution of his purpose. Perceiving that the men were

156

·unable to offer any resistance, he turned his looks on her he valued most. Cora met his gaze with an eye so calm and firm that his resolution wavered. Then, recollecting his former artifice, he raised Alice from the arms of the warrior against whom she leaned, and, beckoning Heyward to follow, he motioned for the encircling crowd to open. But Cora, instead of obeying the impulse he had expected, rushed to the feet of the patriarch, and raising her voice, exclaimed aloud:

'Just and venerable Delaware, on thy wisdom and power we lean for mercy! Be deaf to yonder artful and remorseless monster, who poisons thine ears with falsehoods to feed his thirst for blood. Thou hast lived long and that hast sun the evil of the world, should know how to temper its calamities to the miserable.'

The eyes of the old man opened heavily, and, moving slowly in the direction of the suppliant, finally settled there in a steady gaze. Gradually the expression of Tamenund's features changed, and, losing their vacancy in admiration, they lighted with a portion of that intelligence which a century before had been wont to communicate his youthful fire to the extensive bands of the Delawares. Rising without assistance, and seemingly without an effort, he demanded in a voice that started its auditors by its firmness:

'What art thou?'

'A woman. One of a hated race, if thou wilt — a Yengee. But one who has never harmed thee and who cannot harm thy people, if she would; who ask for succour. Captives against our wills, we have been brought amongst you, and we ask but permission to depart to our own in peace. Let one other speak for us. Let one of thine own people who has not yet been brought before thee be our supplicant. Before thou lettest the Huron depart in triumph, hear him speak.'

Observing Tamenund to look about him doubtingly, one of his companions spoke:

'It is a snake—a redskin in the pay of the Yengeese. We keep him for torture.'

'Let him come,' returned the sage amid a silence so deep that the leaves were distinctly heard rustling in the surrounding forest.

The silence continued unbroken by human sounds for many minutes. Then the waving multitude opened and shut again, and Uncas stood in the living circle. He cast a deliberate and observing look on every side of him, meeting the hostility in the visages of the chiefs with the same calmness as the curious gaze of the attentive children. But when, at last, in his haughty scrutiny, the person of Tamenund came under his glance, his eye became fixed, as though all other objects were already forgotten. Then advancing with a slow and noiseless step up the arena, he placed himself immediately before the footstool of the sage. Here he stood unnoted, though keenly observant himself, until one of the chiefs apprised the latter of his presence.

'With what tongue does the prisoner speak to the Manitto?' demanded the patriarch, without unclosing his eyes.

'Like his fathers,' Uncas replied, 'with the tongue of a Delaware.'

At this sudden and unexpected annunciation a low, fierce yell ran through the multitude. The effect was equally strong on the sage. He passed a hand before his eyes, as if to exclude the least evidence of so shameful a spectacle, while he repeated in low gutteral tones.

'A Delaware! I have seen beasts and birds in the wigwam of man, but never before have I found a Delaware so base as to creep, like a poisonous serpent, into the camps of his nation.'

The sage paused after this outburst and all waited until a movement indicated that he was again to speak.

'Delaware,' resumed the sage, 'little art thou worthy of thy name. My people have not seen a bright sun in many winters, and the warrior who deserts his tribe when hid in clouds is doubly a traitor. The law of the Manitto is just. He is thine, my children. Deal justly by him'.

When the closing syllable of this final decree had passed the lips of Tamenund a cry of vengeance burst at once, as it might be, from the united lips of the nation; a frightful augury of their ruthless intentions. In the midst of these prolonged and savage yells, a chief proclaimed in a high voice that the captive was condemned to endure the dreadful trial of torture by fire. Heyward struggled madly with his captors; the anxious eyes of Hawk-eye began to look around him with an expression of peculiar earnestness; and Cora again threw herself at the feet of the patriarch, once more a suppliant for mercy.

Throughout the whole of these trying moments Uncas had alone preserved his serenity. He looked on the preparations with a steady eye, and when the tormentors came to seize him he met them with a firm and upright attitude. One among them, if possible more fierce and savage than his fellows, seized the hunting shirt of the young warrior, and at a single effort tore it from his body. Then, with a yell of frantic pleasure he leapt towards his unresisting victim and prepared to lead him to the stake. But at that moment, the purpose of the savage was arrested as suddenly as if a supernatural agency had interposed. His eyeballs seemed to start from their sockets, his mouth opened and his raised hand stayed motionless, pointing at the bosom of the captive. His companions, crowded round about him in wonder, and every eye was, like his own, fastened intently on the figure of a small tortoise, beautifully tattooed on the breast of the prisoner, in a bright blue tint.

For a single instant Uncas enjoyed his triumph, smiling calmly on the scene. Then he advanced in front of the nation with the air of a king.

'Men of the Lenni Lenape,' he said, 'my race upholds the earth. Your feeble tribe stands on my shell! What fire that a Delaware can light would burn the child of my fathers?' he added, pointing proudly to the simple blazonry on his skin. 'The blood that came from such a stock would smother your flames. My race is the grandfather of nations.'

'Who art thou?' demanded Tamenund, rising at the startling tones he heard.

'Uncas, the son of Chingachgook,' answered the captive modestly, turning from the nation and bending his head in reverence to the other's character and years, 'A son of the great Unamis—the Turtle.'

'The hour of Tamenund is nigh!' exclaimed the sage. 'The day is come at last to the night! I thank the Manitto that one is here to fill my place at the council fire. Uncas, the child of Uncas, is found! Uncas, the panther of his tribe, the eldest son of Lenape, the wisest Sagamore of the Mohicans! Tell me, ye Delawares, has Tamenund been a sleeper for a hundred winters?'

Uncas, looking in his face with the fondness and veneration of a favoured child, presumed on his own high and acknowledged rank to reply.

'Four warriors of his race have lived and died since the friend of Tamenund led his people in battle. The blood of the turtle has been in many chiefs, but all have gone back into the earth whence they came, except Chingachgook and his son.'

'It is true,' returned the sage. 'Our wise men have often said that two warriors of the unchanged race were in the hills of the Yengeese; why have their seats at the council-fires of the Delawares been so long empty?'

The young man raised his head to explain at once and forever the policy of his family.

'Once we slept where we could hear the salt lake speak in its anger. Then we were rulers and Sagamores over the land. But when a pale-face was seen on every brook, we followed the deer back to the river of our nation. The Delawares were gone. Then said my fathers: "When the Manitto is ready and shall say, 'Come,' we will follow the river to the sea and take our own again." Such, Delawares, is the belief of the children of the Turtle.'

The men of the Lenape listened to his words with all the respect that superstition could lend, finding a secret charm even in the figurative language with which the young Sagamore imparted his ideas. Uncas himself watched the effect of his brief explanation with intelligent eyes, and gradually dropped the air of authority he had assumed as he perceived that his auditors were content. Then, permitting his looks to wander over the silent throng that crowded around the elevated seat of Tamenund, he first perceived Hawk-eye in his bonds. Stepping eagerly from his stand, he made way for himself to the side of his friend, and, cutting his bonds with a quick and angry stroke of his own knife, he motioned to the crowd to divide. The Indians silently obeyed, and once more they stood ranged in their circle, as before, his appearance among them. Uncas took the scout by the hand, and led him to the feet of the patriarch.

'Father, look at this pale-face; a just man and the friend of the Delawares. We call him Hawk-eye, for his sight never fails. The Mingoes know him better as "The Long Rifle."'

'La Longue Carabine!' exclaimed Tamenund. 'My son has not done well to call him friend. The pale-face has slain my young men; his name is great for the blows he has struck the Lenape.'

The scout now believed that is was time for him to vindicate himself. 'That I have slain the Maquas I am not the man to deny, but that, knowingly, my hand has ever harmed a Delaware is opposed to the reason of my gifts, which is friendly to them and all that belongs to their nation.'

A low exclamation of applause passed among the warriors at Hawk-eye's declaration and Uncas knew that the scout's life was no longer in danger.

Magua's feelings during this scene of Uncas' triumph were bitter, indeed, and he now stepped boldly forwards before the patriarch in an attempt to gain his own ends before all was lost.

'The just Tamenund,' he said, 'will not keep what a Huron has lent.'

'Tell me, son of my brother,' returned the sage, avoiding the dark countenance of Le Subtil, and turning gladly to the more ingenuous features of Uncas, 'has the stranger a conqueror's right over you?'

'He has none,' came the reply.

'La Longue Carabine?'

'Laughs at the Mingoes. Go, Huron, ask your squaws the colour of a bear.'

'The stranger and the white maiden that came into my camp together?'

'Should journey on an open path.'

'And the woman that the Huron left with my warriors?'

Uncas made no reply.

'She is mine!' cried Magua, shaking his head in triumph at Uncas. 'Mohican, you know that she is mine.'

'It is so,' was the low answer as the youth turned aside in sorrow.

A short and impressive pause followed, during which it was apparent, with what reluctance the multitude admitted the justice of the Mingo's claim, according to the law of hospitality of the Delawares.

At length the sage, on whom alone the decisions depended, said in a firm voice:

'Huron, depart. Take you the wampum, and our love. Depart with thine own. The great Manitto forbids that a Delaware should be unjust.'

Magua advanced and seized his captive strongly by the arm; and Cora, as if conscious that remonstrance would be useless, prepared to submit to her fate without resistance. Not so her friends.

'Hold, hold!' cried Duncan. 'Huron, have mercy! Her ransom shall make thee richer than any of thy people. Gold, silver, powder, lead—all that a warrior needs shall be in thy wigwam in return for this maiden.'

'Take me in her place,' burst in Hawk-eye, 'me that am a man that it would greatly rejoice your nation to see with naked hands.'

Their appeals were in vain. Magua intimated his contempt of their offers with a backward motion of his head and said in steady and settled voice:

'Le Renard Subtil is a great chief; he has but one mind. Come,' he added, laying his hand too familiarly on the shoulder of his captive, to urge her onward, 'a Huron is no tattler, we will go.'

The maiden drew back in lofty, womanly reserve, and her dark eye kindled, while the rich blood shot, like the passing brightness of the sun, into her very temples at the indignity.

'I am your prisoner, and at a fitting time shall be ready to follow, even to my death. But violence is unnecessary.' she coldly said; and immediately turning to Hawk-eye added; 'Generous hunter, from my soul I thank you. Your offer is vain, neither could it be accepted; but still you may serve me even more than in your own noble intention. Look at that drooping, humbled child! Abandon her not until you leave her in the habitations of civilized men...'

After a long and burning kiss upon her sister's bloodless lips, she arose and turned towards Magua.

'Now, sir, if it be your pleasure I will follow.'

'And I too,' burst out Duncan in despair. 'The Delawares have their laws, which forbid them to detain you, but I have no such obligation. Go, malignant creature, and I following behind will find some way to restore this maiden to her people.'

'Hold,' cried Hawk-eye, detaining Duncan by violence. 'You know not the craft of the imp. He would lead you to an ambushment and your death—'

'Huron,' interrupted Uncas, who, submissive to the stern customs of his people had been an attentive and grave listener to all that passed, 'Huron, the justice of the Delawares comes from the Manitto. Look at the sun. He is now in the upper branches of the hemlock. Your path is short and open. When he is seen above the trees there will be men upon your trail.'

'I hear a crow!' exclaimed Magua with a taunting laugh. 'Go,' he added, shaking his hand at the crowd, which had slowly opened to admit his passage—'Where are the petticoats of the Delawares? Let them send their arrows and their guns to the Wyandots; they shall, have avenison to eat and corn to hoe. Dogs, rabbits thieves,—I spit on you!'

His parting gibes were listened to in a dead boding silence and with these biting words in his mouth, the triumphant Magua passed unmolested into the forest, followed by his passive captive, and protected by the inviolable laws of Indian hospitality.

11

THE LAST OF THE MOHICANS

So long as their enemy and his victim continued in sight, the multitude remained motionless as beings charmed to the place by some power that was friendly to the Huron; but the instant he disappeared it became tossed an agitated by fierce and powerful passion. Uncas maintained his elevated stand, keeping his eyes on the form of Cora until the colours of her dress were blended with the foliage of the forest, then he descended, and, moving silently through the throng, he disappeared in that lodge from which he had so recently issued. During the momentous hour that succeeded the encampment resembled a hive of troubled bees, who only awaited the appearance and example of their leader to take some distant and momentous flight.

When at last the Mohican did reappear, he was divested of all his attire, except his girdle and leggings, and with one half of his fine features hid under a cloud of threatening black. With slow and dignified tread he moved to the tree which, in Indian fashion, had been stripped and painted as indication of a hostile design in the leaders of the nations. Striking his tomahawk deep into the post, he raised his voice in a shout that might be termed his own battle-cry, and the signal awakened all the slumbering passions of the nation. The most ruthless deeds of war were performed on the tree, the fancied emblem of their enemy, with as much ferocity as if it were the living victims of their cruelty. Some were scalped; some received the keen and trembling axe; in short the expedition was declared to be a war of the nation.

The calm but still impatient Uncas now collected his chiefs and divided his power. He presented Hawk-eye as a warrior often tried and always found deserving of confidence. When he found his friend met with a favourable reception, he bestowed on him the command of twenty men, like himself, active, skilful and resolute. He then appointed various native chiefs to fill the different situations of responsability and gave the word to march. He was cheerfully but silently obeyed by more than two hundred men.

Their entrance into the forest was perfectly unmolested, nor did they encounter any living objects that could either give the alarm, or furnish the intelligence they needed, until they came upon the lairs of their own scouts. Here a halt was ordered and the chiefs were assembled to hold a 'whispering council', a practice demanded by custom despite the eagerness of Uncas to rescue the maiden.

During the course of this, a solitary individual was seen advancing from the side of the enemy, with such apparent haste as to induce the belief he might be a messenger charged with pacific overtures. When within a hundred yards of the cover behind which the Delawares council had assembled, however, the stranger hesitated, appearing uncertain what course to take and finally halted.

'His time has come,' said the scout, thrusting the long barrel of his rifle through the leaves; then, instead of pulling the trigger, he lowered the muzzle again and indulged himself in a fit of his peculiar mirth.

'I took the imp for a Mingo,' he said, 'but when my eye ranged along his ribs for a place to get the bullet in—would you think it, Uncas!—I saw the musician's blower. It is the man they call Gamut!'

So saying Hawk-eye crawled through the bushes until within hearing of David and guided him in safety towards the Delawares.

166

'Now give us the history of the Mingo inventions,' he demanded of the musician.

'The heathen are abroad in goodly numbers,' said David, 'and I fear, with evil intent.'

'Where are the Hurons?'

'They lie hid in the forest between this spot and their village, in such force that prudence would teach you instantly to return.'

Uncas cast a glance along the range of trees which concealed his own band and mentioned the name—

'Magua?'

'Is among them. He brought in the maiden that had sojourned with the Delawares, and, leaving her in the cave, has put himself like a raging wolf, at the head of his savages. I know not what has troubled his spirit so greatly.'

'He has left her, you say, in the cave,' interrupted Heyward; ''tis well that we know its situation. May not something be done for her instant relief?'

Uncas looked earnestly at the scout before he asked:

'What says Hawk-eye?'

'Give me my twenty rifles, and I will turn to the right along the stream, and, passing by the huts of the beaver, will join the Sagamore and the colonel. You shall then hear the whoop from that quarter; with this wind one may easily send it a mile. Then, Uncas, do you drive in their front; when they come within range of our pieces we will give them a blow that, I pledge the good name of an old frontiersman, shall make their line bend like an ashen bow. After which we will carry their village and take the woman from the cave, when the affair may be finished with the tribe, according to a white man's battle, by a blow and a victory, or, in the Indian fashion, with dodge and cover. There may be no great learning, Major, in this plan, but with courage and patience, it can all be done.'

'I like it much,' cried Duncan, who saw that the release of Cora was the primary object in the mind of the scout; 'I like it much. Let it be instantly attempted.'

Hawk-eye, when he saw his little band collected, threw 'Kill-deer' into the hollow of his arm and making a silent signal that he would be followed, he led them many rods towards the rear, into the bed of a little brook which they had crossed in advancing. Here he halted, and after waiting for the whole of his grave and attentive warriors to close about him, he spoke in Delaware, demanding:

'Do any of my young men know whither this run will lead us?'

A Delaware stretched forth a hand, with the two fingers separated, and, indicating the manner in which they were joined at the root, he answered:

'Before the sun could go his own length the little water will be in the big.' Then he added, pointing in the direction of the place he mentioned: 'The two make enough for the beavers.'

'I thought as much,' returned the scout, glancing his eye upwards at the opening in the tree-tops, 'from the course it takes and the bearings of the mountains. Men, we will keep within the cover of its banks till we scent the Hurons.'

Their route lay, for the distance of a mile, along the bed of the watercourse. Though protected from any great danger of observation by the precipitous banks and the thick shrubbery which skirted the stream, no precaution known to an Indian attack was neglected. Their march was, however, unmolested and they reached the point where the lesser stream was lost in the greater, without the smallest evidence that their progress had been noted. Here the scout again halted to consult the signs of the forest.

He knew that the Huron encampment lay a short halfmile up the brook, and, with the characteristic anxiety of one who dreaded a hidden danger, he was greatly troubled at not finding the smallest trace of the presence of his enemy. Once or twice he felt induced to give the order for a rush, and to attempt the village by surprise, but his experience admonished him of the danger of so useless an experiment. Then he listened intently and with painful uncertainty for the sounds of hostility in the quarter where Uncas was left; but nothing was audible but the sighing of the wind, that began to sweep over the bosom of the forest in gusts which threatened a tempest. At length, yielding rather to his unusual impatience than taking counsel from his knowledge he determined to bring matters to an issue by unmasking his force and proceeding cautiously, but steadily, up the stream. Quickly he gave the signal for the whole party to steal up the bank and follow him in single file.

The party was, however, scarcely uncovered before a volley from a dozen rifles was heard in their rear, and a Delaware, leaping high into the air, like a wounded deer, fell at his full length, perfectly dead.

'Ah! I feared some devilry like this!' exclaimed the scout in English; adding with the quickness of thought, in his adopted tongue: 'To cover men, and charge!'

The band dispersed at the word, and the scout set the example of pressing on their retreat, by discharging his rifle and darting from tree to tree, as his enemy slowly yielded ground.

It would seem that the assault had been made by a very small party of Hurons, which, however, continued to increase in numbers as it retired on its friends, until the return fire was very nearly, if not quite, equal to that maintained by the advancing Delawares. Heyward threw himself among the combatants, and, imitating, the necessary caution of his companions, he made quick discharges with his own rifle. The contest now grew warm and stationary. Few were injured as both parties kept their bodies as much protected as possible by the trees, never, indeed, exposing any part of their persons except in the act of taking aim. But Hawk-eye saw it was more dangerous to retreat than to maintain his ground, while he found his enemy throwing out men on his flank, which rendered the task of keeping themselves covered so very difficult to the Delawares as nearly to silence their fire. At this embarassing moment when they began to think the

169

whole hostile tribe was gradually encircling them, they heard the yell of combatants and the rattling of arms echoing under the arches of the wood at the place where Uncas was posted. It would seem that while Hawk-eye's own surprise had been anticipated, and had consequently failed, the enemy, in their turn, having been deceived in its object and in his numbers, had left too small a force to resist the impetuous onset of the young Mohican, as was apparent by the rapid manner in which the battle in the forest now rolled upwards towards the village.

Animating his followers by his voice and his own example, Hawk-eye then gave the word to bear down on their foes. The charge, in that rude species of warfare, consisted in merely pushing from cover to cover, nigher to the enemy; and in this manœuvre he was instantly and successfully obeyed. The Hurons were compelled to withdraw, and the scene of the contest rapidly charged from the more open ground on which it had commenced to a spot where the assailed found a thicket to rest upon. Without stopping to breathe the Delawares leapt in long bounds towards the woods like so many panthers springing upon their prey, and swept away every trace of resistance by the fury of the onset.

The assailed yielded ground rapidly, until they reached the opposite margin of the thicket, where they clung to the cover with the sort of obstinacy that is so often witnessed in hunted brutes. At this critical moment when the success of the struggle was again becoming doubtful, the crack of a bullet was heard behind the Hurons, and a bullet came whizzing from among some beaver lodges which were situated in the clearing in their rear, and was followed by the fierce and appalling yell of the war-whoop.

'There speaks the Sagamore!' shouted Hawk-eye answering the cry with his own stentorian voice. 'We have them now in face and back!'

The effect on the Hurons was instantaneous. Discouraged by an assault from a quarter that left them no opportunity for cover, their warriors uttered a common yell of disappointment, and breaking off in a body, they spread themselves across the opening, heedless of every consideration but flight. Many fell, in making the experiment, under the bullets and the blows of the pursuing Delawares.

We shall not pause to detail the meeting between the scout and Chingachgook, or the more touching interview that Duncan held with Munro. A few brief and hurried words served to explain the state of things to both parties, and then Hawk-eye, pointing out the Sagamore to his band, resigned the chief authority into the hands of the Mohican chief. Chingachgook assumed the station to which his birth and experience gave him so distinguished a claim, and, following the footsteps of the scout, he led the party back through the thicket, his own men scalping the fallen Hurons, and secreting the bodies of their own dead as they proceeded until they gained a point where the former was content to make a halt.

The warriors were now posted on a bit of level ground sprinkled with trees in sufficient numbers to conceal them. The land fell away rather precipitately in front, and beneath their eyes, stretched for several miles, a narrow, dark and wooded vale. The Mohican and his friends advanced to the brow of the hill and listened with practised ears to the sounds of the combat. It was clear to them that it was through this dense and dark forest that Uncas was still contending with the main body of the Hurons.

'The fight is coming up the ascent,' said Duncan, pointing in the direction of a new explosion of firearms. 'We are too much in the centre of their line to be effective.'

'They will incline into the hollow where the cover is thicker,' said the scout, 'and that will leave us well on their flank. Go, Sagamore, it is for you to watch the issue and to give to whoop that will lead on the young men. I will fight this scrimmage with warriors of my own colour. You know me, Mohican; not a Huron of them all shall cross the swell into your rear without the notice of "Kill-deer".'

The Indian chief paused to consider the signs of the contest, which was now rolling rapidly up the ascent, a certain evidence that the Delawares triumphed. Hawkeye and his three companions withdrew a few paces to a shelter, and awaited the issue with calmness that nothing but great practice could impart in such a scene.

It was not long before the reports of the rifles began to lose the echoes of the woods, and to sound like weapons discharged in the open air. Then a warrior appeared here and there, driven to the skirts of the forest and rallying as he entered the clearing, as at the place where the final stand was to be made. These were soon joined by others, until a long line of swarthy figures was to be seen clinging to the cover with the obstinacy of desperation. Heyward began to grow impatient, and turned his eyes anxiously in the direction of Chingachgook, still seated on a rock as if he were posted there merely to view the struggle.

'The time is come for the Delaware to strike!' said Duncan.

'Not so, not so,' returned the scout. 'When he scents his friends, he will let them know that he is here.'

Even as he spoke, the whoop was given, and a dozen Hurons fell from a discharge from Chingachgook and his band. The shout that followed was answered by a single war-cry from the forest, and a yell passed through the air that sounded as if a thousand throats were united in a common effort. The Hurons staggered, deserting the centre of their line, and Uncas issued from the forest, through the opening they left at the head of a hundred warriors.

Waving his hands right and left, the young chief pointed out the enemy to his followers, who separated in pursuit. The war now divided, both wings of the broken Hurons seeking protection in the woods again, hotly pressed by the victorious warriors of the Lenape. One little knot of Hurons, however, had disdained to seek cover, and were retiring like lions at bay, slowly and sullenly up the acclivity which Chingachgook and his band had just deserted to mingle more closely in the fray. Magua was conspicuous in this party, both by his fierce and savage mien and by the air of haughty authority he yet maintained.

In his eagerness to expedite the pursuit, Uncas had left himself nearly alone; but the moment his eye caught the figure of Le Subtil, every other consideration was forgotten. Raising his cry of battle, which recalled some six or seven warriors, and reckless of the disparity of their numbers, he rushed upon his enemy. Le Renard, who watched the movement, paused to receive him with secret joy. But at the moment when he thought the rashness of his impetuous young assailant had left him at his mercy, another shout was given, and La Longue Carabine was seen rushing to the rescue, attended by all his white associates. The Huron instantly turned and commenced a rapid retreat up the ascent.

There was no time for greetings or congratulations, for Uncas, though conscious of the presence of his friends, continued the pursuit with the velocity of the wind. In vain Hawk-eye called to him to respect the covers; the young Mohican braved the dangerous fire of his enemies, and soon compelled them to a flight as swift as his own headlong speed. Pursuers and pursued thus entered the Wyandot village within striking distance of each other.

Excited by the presence of their dwellings and tired of the chase, the Hurons now made a stand, and fought around their council lodge with the fury of despair. The tomahawk of Uncas, the blows of Hawk-eye, and even the still nervous arm of Munro were all busy for that passing moment, and the ground was quickly strewed with their enemies. Still Magua, though daring and much exposed, escaped from every effort against his life, with that sort of fabled protection that was made to overlook the fortunes of favoured heroes in the legends of ancient poetry.

Raising a yell that spoke volumes of anger and disappointment, the subtle chief, when he saw his comrades fallen, darted away from the place, attended by his two only surviving friends, leaving the Delawares engaged in stripping the dead of the bloody trophies of their victory.

But Uncas, who had vainly sought him in the mêlée, bounded forward in pursuit, Hawk-eye and Heyward still pressing on his footsteps. Once Magua appeared disposed to make another attempt to revenge his losses, but abandoning his intention he suddenly entered the mouth of the cave already known to the reader. As the pursuers dashed into the long and narrow entrance in time to catch a glimpse of the retreating forms of the Hurons, it was only in tenderness to Uncas that Hawk-eye forbore to fire, for well he knew that Le Subtil must be the Mohican's own prize.

Still Uncas kept his eye on Magua as if life to him possessed but a single object. Heyward and the scout still pressed on his rear, actuated, though possibly in a less degree, by a common feeling. But their way was becoming intricate in those dark and gloomy passages and the glimpses of the retiring warriors less distinct and frequent; and for some moment the trace was believed to be lost, when a white robe was seen fluttering in the farthest extremity of a passage that seemed to lead up a mountain.

"'Tis Cora!' exclaimed Heyward in a voice in which horror and delight were wildly mingled.

'Cora! Cora!' echoed Uncas, bending forward like a deer.

"'Tis the maiden!' shouted the scout. 'Courage, lady; we come, we come!'

The chase was renewed with a diligence rendered tenfold encouraging by this glimpse of the captive. But the way was rugged and broken, and to ease their passage first Uncas, then Heyward abandoned their rifles and leaped forward with headlong precipitation. Both were, a moment afterwards, admonished of this madness by hearing the bellowing of a piece down the passage in the rocks, the bullet from which gave the young Mohican a slight wound.

'We must close!' said the scout, passing his friends by a desperate leap. 'The knaves will pick us all off at this distance; and see, they hold the maiden so as to shield themselves!'

Though his words were unheeded, or rather unheard, his example was followed by his companions, who by incredible exertions, got near enough to the fugitives to perceive that Cora was borne along between the two warriors, while Magua prescribed the direction and manner of their flight. At this moment the forms of all were drawn strongly against an opening in the sky, and they disappeared. Nearly frantic with disappointment, Uncas and Heyward increased efforts that already seemed superhuman, and they issued from the cabin on the side of the mountain, in time to note the route of the pursued. The course lay up the ascent, and still continued hazardous and laborious.

Encumbered by his rifle, the scout suffered his companions to precede him a little, Uncas in his turn taking the lead of Heyward. But the impetuous young men were rewarded by finding that, encumbered with Cora, the Hurons were losing ground in the race.

'Stay, dog of the Wyandots', exclaimed Uncas, shaking his bright tomahawk at Magua; 'a Delaware girl calls you to stay!'

'I will go no farther,' cried Cora, stopping unexpectedly on a ledge of rocks that overhung a deep precipice, at no great distance from the summit of the mountain. 'Kill me if thou wilt, detestable Huron, I will go no farther.'

For answer, the Huron chief drew his knife, and turned to his captive with a look in which conflicting passions fiercely contended.

'Woman,' he said, 'choose: the wigwam or the knife of Le Subtil.'

175

Cora regarded him not, but, dropping on her knees, she raised her eyes and stretched her arms towards heaven, saying in a meek and yet confiding voice:

'I am thine! Do with me as thou seest best!'

'Woman,' repeated Magua hoarsely, and endeavouring in vain to catch a glance from her serene and beaming eye, 'choose!'

Just then a piercing cry was heard above them and Uncas appeared, leaping frantically from a fearful height upon the ledge. Magua recoiled a step, and in the brief interval that followed, one of his assistants, profiting by the chance, sheathed his own knife in the bosom of Cora.

The Huron sprang like a tiger on his murderous countryman, but the falling form of Uncas separated the unnatural combatants. Diverted from his object by this interruption, and maddened by the murder he had just witnessed, Magua buried his weapon in the back of the prostrate Delaware, uttering an unearthly shout as he committed the destardly deed. But Uncas arose from the blow, as the wounded panther turns upon his foe, and struck the murderer of Cora to his feet by an effort in which the last of his failing strength was expended. Then, with a stern and steady look he turned to Le Subtil, and indicated by the expression of his eye all that he would do had not the power deserted him. The latter seized the nerveless arm of the unresisting Delaware and passed his knife into his bosom several times before his victim, still keeping his gaze riveted on his enemy with a look of inextinguishable scorn, fell dead at his feet.

'Mercy! Mercy, Huron!' cried Heyward from above in tones nearly choked by horror. 'Give mercy and thou shalt receive it!'

Whirling the bloody knife up at the imploring youth, the victorious Magua uttered a cry so fierce, so wild; and yet so joyous that it conveyed the sounds of savage triumph to the ears of those who fought in the valley a thousand feet below. He was answered by a burst from the lips of the scout, whose tall person was just then seen moving swiftly towards him along those dangerous crags, with steps as bold and reckless as if he possessed the power to move in air; but when the hunter reached the scene of the ruthless massacre the ledge was tenanted only by the dead.

His keen eye took a single look at the victims, and then shot its glances over the difficulties of the ascent in his front. Far ahead Magua issued from a crevice and ascended the rocks at a point whence a single bound would carry him to the brow of the precipice and assure his safety. Before taking the leap, however, the Huron paused, and shaking his hand at the scout, he shouted:

'The pale-faces are dogs! the Delawares women! Magua leaves them on the rocks for the crows!'

Laughing hoarsely he made a desperate leap, and 'ell short of his mark, though his hands grasped a hrub on the verge of the height. Without exhausting imself with fruitless efforts, the cunning Magua uffered his body to drop to the length of his arms, nd found a fragment for his feet to rest on. Then, summoning all his powers, he renewed the attempt, and so far succeeded as to draw his knees on the edge of the mountain. It was now, when the body of his enemy was most collected together, that the weapon of the scout was drawn to his shoulder. The surrounding rocks themselves were not steadier than the piece became for the single instant that it poured out its contents. The arms of the Huron relaxed, and his body fell back a little, while his knees still kept their position. Turning a relentless look on his enemy, he shook a hand in grim defiance. But his hold loosened and his dark person was seen cutting the air, with its head downwards for a fleeting instant, until it glided past the fringe of shrubbery which clung to the mountain, in its rapid flight to destruction.

The sun found the Lenape, on the succeeding day, a nation of mourners. The sounds of the battle were over and they had paid their ancient grudge, but no shouts of success, no songs of triumph, were heard in rejoicing for their victory. The lodges were deserted, but a broad belt of earnest faces encircled a spot in their vicinity whither everything possessing life had repaired, and where all were now collected in deep and awful silence. Each eye was riveted on the centre of that ring, which contained the objects of so much and of so common an interest.

Six Delaware girls, with their long, dark flowing tresses falling loosely across their bosoms, stood apart, strewing sweet-scented herbs and forest flowers on a litter of fragrant plants that, under a pall of Indian robes, supported all that now remained of the high-souled and generous Cora. Her form was concealed in many wrappers of the same simple manufacture, and her face was shut for ever from the gaze of men. At her feet was seated the desolate Munro, his aged head bowed nearly to the earth in compelled submission to the stroke of Providence, while his eyes, wandering and concerned, seemed to be equally divided between that little volume, which contained so many quaint but holy, maxims, and the being in whose behalf his soul yearned to administer consolation. Heyward was also nigh, supporting himself against a tree, and endeavouring to keep down those sudden risings of sorrow that it required his utmost manhood to subdue.

But, sad and melancholy as this group may easily be imagined, it was far less touching than another that occupied the opposite space on the same area. Seated, as in life, with his form and limbs arranged in grave and decent composure, the body of Uncas appeared arrayed in the most gorgeous ornaments that the wealth of the tribe could furnish. Rich plumes nodded above his head; wampum, gorgets, bracelets and medals adorned his person in profusion. Directly in front of the corpse Chingachgook was placed, without arms, paint or adornment of any sort, except the bright blue blazonry of his race that was indelibly impressed on his naked bosom. During the long period the tribe had been thus collected, the Mohican warrior had kept such a riveted and intense gaze on the senseless countenance of his son that a stranger might not have told the living from the dead but for the occasional gleamings of the eyes.

The scout was hard by, leaning in a pensive posture on his own fatal and avenging weapon; while Tamenund, supported by the elders of his nation, occupied a high place at hand, whence he might look down on the mute and sorrowful assemblage of his people.

The multitude had maintained its breathing stillness from the dawn of the day until the closing of its first quarter when at length the sage of the Delawares stretched forth an arm, and, leaning on the shoulders of his attendants, he arose and tottered on his elevated stand.

'Men of the Lenape!' he said in hollow tones that sounded like a voice charged with some prophetic mission; 'the face of the Manitto is behind a cloud; his eye is turned from you, his ears are shut, his tongue gives no answer. You see him not, yet his judgements are before you. Let your hearts be open and your spirits tell no lie. Men of the Lenape, the face of the Manitto is behind a cloud.'

As this simple yet terrible annunciation stole on the ears of the multitude, a low murmur of voices commenced a sort of chant in honour of the dead. The thrillingly soft and wailing sounds were those of females, who called him the 'panther of the tribe' and described him as one whose moccasins left no trail on the dews, whose bound was like the leap of the young fawn, whose eye was brighter than a star in the dark night, and whose voice in battle was loud as the thunder of the Manitto.

Others dwelt upon the matchless beauty and noble resolution of the stranger maiden and recommended her to the protection and companionship of the manly and generous Mohican whose departure from the upper earth at the same time as her own could be regarded only as the will of the Great Spirit that they should be joined in their future existence.

The scout, to whom alone of all the white men the words were intelligible, bent his head aside to catch their meaning as the girls proceeded. But when they spoke of the future prospects of Cora and Uncas, he shook his head like one who knew the error of their simple creed. Happily for the self command of both Heyward and Munro, they knew nothing of the meaning of the wild sounds they heard.

Chingachgook was a solitary exception to the interest manifested by the native part of the audience. No muscle moved in his rigid countenance, even at the wildest or the most pathetic parts of the lamentation. The cold and senseless remains of his son was all to him, and every other sense but that of sight seemed frozen, in order that his eyes might take their final gaze at those lineaments he had so long loved, and which were now about to be closed forever from his view.

Only after most of the high and gifted men of the nation had sung their tribute of praise over the deceased chief, did the lips of Chingachgook so tar part as to announce that it was the monody of the father. The multitude drank in the sounds with an intenseness of attention that none but Tamenund himself had ever before commanded; but they listened in vain. The strains rose just so loud as to become intelligible and then grew fainter and more trembling, until they finally sank on the ear, as if borne away by a passing breath of wind. The lips of the Sagamore closed and he • remained silent in his seat, looking, with his riveted eye and motionless form, like some creature that had been turned from the Almighty hand with the form but without the spirit of a man. The Delawares, who knew by these symptoms that the mind of their friend was not prepared for so mighty an effort of fortitude, relaxed in their attention, and, with an innate delicacy, seemed to bestow all their thoughts on the obsequies of the stranger maiden.

A signal was given by one of the elder chiefs to the women, who crowded that part of the circle near which the body of Cora lay. Obedient to the sign, the girls raised the bier to the elevation of their heads, and advanced with slow and regulated steps, chanting as they proceeded another wailing song in praise of the deceased. Gamut who had been a close observer of rites he deemed so heathenish, now bent his head over the shoulder of the unconscious father, whispering:

'They move with the remains of thy child; shall we not follow and see them interred with Christian burial?'

Munro started, as if the last trumpet had sounded in his ear, and arose and followed in the simple train, with the mien of a soldier, but bearing the full burden of a parent's suffering. His friends pressed around him with a sorrow that was too strong to be termed sympathy. But when the last and humblest female of the tribe had joined in the wild and yet ordered array, the men of the Lenape contracted their circle, and formed again around the person of Uncas, as silent, as grave and as motionless as before.

The place which had been chosen for the grave of Cora was a little knoll, where a cluster of young and beautiful pines had taken root, forming themselves a melancholy and appropriate shade over the spot. On reaching it the girls deposited their burden, waiting with characteristic patience and native timidity for some evidence that they whose feelings were most concerned were content with the arrangement. At length, the scout, who alone understood their habits, said in their own language:

'My daughters have done well; the white men thank them.'

Satisfied with this testimony in their favour, the girls proceeded to deposit the body in a shell, ingeniously and not inelegantly fabricated of the bark of the birch; after which they lowered it into its dark and final abode. The ceremony of covering the remains, and concealing the marks of the fresh earth by leaves and other natural and customary objects, was conducted with the same simple and silent forms. When the labours of the kind beings who had performed these sad and friendly offices were so far completed, the scout again addressed them:

'My young women have done enough', he said. 'The spirit of a pale-face has no need of food or raiment—their gifts being according to the heaven of their colour. I see,' he added, glancing an eye at David, who was preparing his book in a manner that indicated his intention to lead the way in sacred song, 'that one who better knows the Christian fashions is about to speak.'

The females stood modestly aside, and from having been the principal actors in the scene they now became the meek and attentive observers of that which followed. During the time David was occupied in pouring out the pious feelings of his spirit in this manner, not a sign of surprise nor look of impatience escaped them. They listened like those who knew the meaning of the strange words, and appeared as if they felt the mingled emotions of sorrow, hope and resignation they were intended to convey.

When, the closing cadence had fallen on the ears of his auditors, Munro bared his grey locks and looked around the timid and quiet throng, by which he was encircled, with a firm and collected countenance. Then, motioning with his hand for the scout to listen, he said:

'Say to these kind and gentle females that a heart-broken and failing man returns them his thanks.'

Turning to the women, the scout communicated the other's gratitude; then, seeing that the head of Munro had already sunk upon his chest in renewed melancholy, he drew the attention of the mourning old man towards a group of young Indians, who approached with a light but closely-covered litter, and then pointed towards the sun.

'I understand you, sir,' returned Munro, with a voice of forced firmness; 'I understand you. It is the will of heaven, and I submit. Cora, my child, if the prayers of a heartbroken father could avail thee now, how blessed shouldst thou be! Come, gentlemen,' he added, looking about him with an air of lofty composure, though the anguish that quivered in his faded countenance was far too powerful to be concealed, 'our duty here is ended. Let us depart.'

Heyward gladly obeyed a summons that took them from a spot where, each instant, he felt his self-control was about to desert him. While his companions were mounting, however, he found time to press the hand of the scout, and to repeat the terms of an engagement they had made to meet again within the posts of the British Army. Then, gladly throwing himself into the saddle, he spurred his charger to the side of the litter, where low and stifled sobs alone announced the presence of Alice. In this manner, the head of Munro again dropping on his bosom, with Heyward and David following in sorrowful silence, all the white men, with the exception of Hawk-eye, passed from before the eyes of the Delawares, and were soon buried in the vast forests of that region.

But the tie which, through their common calamity, had united the feelings of these simple dwellers in the woods with the strangers who had thus transiently visited them was not so easily broken. Years passed away before the traditionary tale of the white maiden and of the young warrior of the Mohicans ceased to beguile the long nights and tedious marches, or to animate their youthful and brave with a desire for vengeance. Neither were the secondary actors in these momentous incidents forgotten. Through the medium of the scout, who served for years afterwards as a link between them and civilized life, they learned in answer to their inquiries that the 'Grey Head' was speedily gathered to his fathers—borne down, as was erroneously believed by his military misfortunes; and that the 'Open Hand' had conveyed his only surviving daughter far into the settlements of the pale-faces, where at last her tears had ceased to flow, and had been succeeded by the bright smiles which were better suited to her joyous nature.

But these were events of a time later than that which concerns our tale. Deserted by all of his colour, Hawkeye returned to the spot where his own sympathies led him with a force that no ideal bond of union could bestow. He was just in time to catch a parting look at the features of Uncas, whom the Delawares were already enclosing in his last vestments of skins. They paused to permit the longing and lingering gaze of the sturdy woodsman, and when it had ended, the body was enveloped, never to be enclosed again.

The movement, like the feeling, had been simultaneous and general. The same grave expressions of grief, the same rigid silence and the same deference to the principal mourner were observed around the place of interment as has been already described. The body was deposited in an attitude of repose, facing the rising sun, with the implements of war and of the chase at hand, in readiness for the final journey. An opening was left in the shell by which it was protected from the soil, for the spirit to communicate with its earthly tenement when necessary, and the whole was concealed from the instinct, and protected from the ravages of the beasts of prey, with an ingenuity peculiar to the natives. The manual rites then ceased, and all present reverted to the more spiritual part of the ceremonies.

Chingachgook once more became the object of the common attention. He had not yet spoken and something consolatory and instructive was expected from so renowned a chief on such an occasion of such interest. Conscious of the wishes of the people, the stern and self-restrained warrior raised his face, which had latterly been buried in his robe, and looked about him with a steady eye. His firmly compressed and expressive lips then severed, and for the first time during the long ceremonies his voice was distinctly audible.

'Why do my brothers mourn?' he said regarding the dark race of dejected warriors by whom he was environed. 'Why do my daughters weep? That a young man has gone to the happy hunting grounds? That a chief has filled his time with honour? He was good, he was dutiful, he was brave! Who can deny it? The Manitto had need of such a warrior, and he has called him away. As for me, the son and father of Uncas, I am a blazed pine in a clearing of the palefaces. My race has gone from the shores of the salt lake and the hills of the Delawares. But who can say that the serpent of his tribe has forgotten his wisdom? I am alone...'

'No, no!' cried Hawk-eye, who had been gazing with a yearning look at the rigid features of his friend, with something like his own self-command, but whose philosophy could endure no longer; 'no, Sagamore, not alone. The gifts of our colours may be different, but God has placed us as to journey in the same path. I have no kin, and I may also say, like you, no people. He was your son and a redskin by nature, and it may be that your blood was nearer; but if ever I forget the lad who has so often fou't at my side in war, and slept at my side in peace, may He who made us all, whatever be our colour or our gifts, forget me. The boy has left us for a time, but, Sagamore, you are not alone.'

Chingachgook grasped the hand that in the warmth of feeling, the scout had stretched across the fresh earth, and in that attitude of friendship these two sturdy and intrepid woodsmen bowed their heads together, while scalding tears fell to their feet, watering the grave of Uncas like drops of falling rain.

In the midst of the awful stillness with which such a burst of feeling, coming, as it did, from the two most renowned warriors of that region, was received, Tamenund lifted his voice to disperse the multitude.

185

'It is enough', he said. 'Go, children of the Lenape, the anger of the Manitto is not done. Why should Tamenund stay? The pale-faces are the masters of the earth, and the time of the red man has not come again. My day has been too long. In the morning I saw the sons of Unamis happy and strong; and yet, before the night has come, have I lived to see the last warrior of the wise race of the Mohicans.'

PRINTED IN ROMANIA

Abbey